Missionary Position

Masters of the Prairie Winds Club
Book Seven

by Avery Gale

Copyright © October 2015 by Avery Gale
ISBN 978-1-944472-16-0
All cover art and logo © Copyright 2015 by Avery Gale
All rights reserved.

The Masters of the Prairie Winds Club® and Avery Gale®
are registered trademarks

Cover Design by Jess Buffett
Published by Avery Gale

Thank you for respecting the hard work of this author.

This is a work of fiction. Names, places, characters and incidents either are the product of the author's imagination or are used fictitiously and any resemblance to any actual persons, living or dead, organizations, events or locales are entirely coincidental.

No part of this book may be reproduced, stored in a retrieval system, or transmitted by any means without the written permission of the author and publishing company.

WARNING: The unauthorized reproduction or distribution of this copyrighted work is illegal. Criminal copyright infringement, including infringement without monetary gain, is investigated by the FBI and is punishable by up to 5 years in federal prison and a fine of $250,000.

If you find any books being sold or shared illegally, please contact the author at avery.gale@ymail.com.

Dedication

There are times in your life when the most important lessons are taught by people who are really good bad examples…my wish for you is that you are blessed with loyal friends and family, and your encounters with "bad apples" are few and far between.

Chapter One

Lara Emmons quietly took her place between Peter and Fischer Weston smiling to herself because they'd both taken a step to the side making room for her despite the fact she knew they hadn't actually seen her come in behind them. It always amazed her when they sensed her approach. They had been standing shoulder to shoulder when she'd stepped silently into the room, but they had each taken a single step in opposite directions before she'd even closed the door behind her. Dressed in matching all black tuxes, the two men were mouth-wateringly gorgeous. It still took her breath away at times when she looked at them. And knowing all the delights hidden below those dapper garments? Holy craptastic capers, Batman, just standing close to them was enough to make a girl swoon.

Trying not to snicker at her melodramatic thoughts—damn she really did need to stop watching late night television—Lara focused on the fact that even though both men were Doms, they didn't let it keep them from being courteous to everyone they came into contact with. And speaking of contact—sweet God in heaven their touch, even the casual way they were carefully maintaining contact from shoulders to hips was sending shivers up and down her spine. Lara loved the feeling of being cossetted between them. The warmth from their bodies almost made up for the next-to-nothing dress the two of them had chosen for her to wear, even standing perfectly still the hem barely covered the bottom curve of her ass cheeks. Lara was grateful the reception was inside because the slightest breeze was sure to move the *almost* translucent fabric, exposing her bare girly bits to every guest in the room. And while it was true most of the people here were members of Dark Desires, there were still several from the vanilla world who might not think seeing her pink bits was appropriate. Squirming at the thought, Lara gasped when Fischer gave her a quick swat, "Stop squirming, cupcake."

Yes, sireee, it was just like the man to wait until there was nothing between her ass and his hand but a handful of threads to become completely focused on every move she made. Lara had spent months trying to tempt Fischer into touching her, and just when she'd finally resigned herself to the fact he wasn't interested, everything changed.

Fischer Weston had been Cameron Barnes' second-in-command but had taken the helm at Dark Desires after Cam decided to move his family to St. Maarten. Shortly before the Barnes moved, Fischer's brother, Peter, had been dispatched to help secure the club following threats to CeCe, and Lara learned quickly why Fischer had been holding back. Now, Kyle and Kent West were purchasing Dark Desires, and both Weston brothers were acting as managers. The three of them had been living in the Barnes' former penthouse apartment and Lara marveled every day at how much her life had changed in such a short time.

Mentally shaking her head as she remembered how often she'd dreamed of being naked and at Fischer's mercy before it had become a reality. Lara thought back on how the handsome Dom had nearly driven her out of her mind with his attention and flirting—always close, but just out of reach. She'd been able to *see* his interest, but he'd always stopped just short of pushing it further and Lara had wondered a thousand times what she was doing wrong. She could still remember every detail about the first time they met, it was the day she'd finally gotten up the nerve to step through the front doors of Dark Desires and inquire about membership.

It had taken her weeks to get up the courage to track down the kink club she'd heard so much about and then even longer to have the nerve to actually decide to visit. Hell, she had made several attempts before actually making her way inside. During the first few forays, she hadn't even made it past the gatehouse at the street. It was a miracle the security guard working in the small building hadn't called the police…hell, it was a wonder he hadn't dropped a net over her until the local mental health hospital could dispatch the white coat brigade to retrieve her. She'd known he watched her pace up and down the sidewalk trying desperately to work up the nerve to request admittance, she'd even seen him trying to suppress a smile a time or two. After she'd gotten a job at the club, he'd teased her about her reluctance and when she'd flushed in mortification he'd given her a solid swat welcoming her to the fun side of town.

She'd been wearing a floral sundress the day her curiosity and desire had finally won out over her fear—good Lord, she must have looked like Alice in Wonderland. Walking though the heavy engraved doors had certainly been akin to stepping through the looking glass because her entire life had changed for forever in that moment. And now, looking back, she couldn't help but shake her head at what everyone had to have thought because she had to have looked like the poster child for bimbo tourists everywhere. But the sad truth was she'd been trying to impress everyone by dressing up in her nicest clothes. The children of missionaries didn't have enormous clothing allowances and the simple sundress she'd worn had been the single piece in her wardrobe that hadn't been washed a zillion times.

By the time she'd made her way past the gatehouse and down the long drive leading to the club itself to step into the lavishly decorated reception area, Lara had been shaking so badly she'd worried her knees were actually going to start knocking against one another. But if she'd thought working up her nerve to enter had been tough, the worst was yet to come. Hearing the exorbitant membership cost had been earth shattering—all those weeks of anticipation had paled in the disillusionment she'd felt. Even though she'd tried to cover up her disappointment, she'd seen the knowing looks in the eyes of those watching her with a mixture of surprise and disdain that someone who was so obviously an outsider had even entertained the idea she might be able to join. Oh yeah, the people standing in the opulent entry hadn't been fooled by her quick nod of understanding and polite thanks as she backed toward the door. She'd almost made it to the exit and she was proud of herself for holding back the tears of humiliation threatening to steal the last bits of her shredded dignity. Why she'd thought she had a prayer of being able to afford a membership had been a mystery.

Lara had been shocked when the incredibly handsome man who'd been standing to the side of the reception desk spoke up. He was without any doubt the best looking man she'd ever seen, his movie star looks had stolen her ability to focus and when he stepped around the chest high counter to stand in front of her, the only thing Lara had been able to do was stare up at him. She had probably looked even more like a fish out of water standing there with her mouth hanging open. He'd introduced himself and mentioned a program the club's owner was considering, which would allow potential members the opportunity to work part-time in one of the small businesses being opened inside the club in exchange for a reduction of their membership fee. Lara hadn't known until recently that Fischer's motives had been far from altruistic.

Listening to the ceremony taking place across the large room, Lara couldn't hold back her giddiness as she watched her former boss and his wife recommit themselves to one another before they each in turn pledged themselves to Carl Phillips. Seeing the love so clearly written in their expressions and watching how effortlessly it flowed between the three of them renewed her hope of someday finding the same joy. And knowing the unique dynamics of their relationship made Lara smile. Their extraordinary relationship was a perfect reminder that love doesn't always look like we expect it to. That lesson in tolerance had been one her missionary parents had impressed upon her repeatedly when she was younger. As she'd grown up, Lara had gradually realized Lawrence and Rita Emmons methods of teaching Biblical lessons was more political and action based—something she assumed was part of the reason they were transferred so often.

Her mom and dad had taken various missionary positions around the globe, and had only settled in Texas to fulfill a promise they'd made years earlier. Allowing their daughter to complete high school in one place had been an enormous concession on their part, but Lara had made the deal with them when she'd been too young to understand the challenge it presented to them, but she had to admire the fact they'd kept their word. Her mom and dad might not have been considered Evangelicals completely devoted to spreading the word of God, but that didn't mean they'd forgotten the fact unconditional love was at the core of their religious beliefs. Lara had lived in some of the most poverty stricken and politically volatile areas of the world, where her blond hair and curvy figure drew a lot of negative attention. But her parents had always stressed the importance of being true to yourself, and it had been that particular lesson that had given her the courage to explore the piece of sexuality that didn't seem to fit in with her friends' views.

Bringing her attention back to the moment, Lara admired the transformation Tobi West and Gracie McDonald had made in the club's main room. The entire event had been organized by the two whirlwinds from The Prairie Winds Club and they had somehow turned the kink club's largest room into something resembling an English garden. How they had managed to use so many flowers baffled Lara and the crew that had carried in case after case of every imaginable type of flora. As she stood between Peter and Fischer Weston, she felt her heart melting at the intimacy of the ceremony itself. Tobi and Gracie might have done everything else, but the vows had obviously been written by the participants themselves. The ceremony was being conducted by a member of the club, and even though Cam and CeCe were still the only ones legally married, Lara would defy anyone to deny unity of all three people making their pledges to one another.

Over the past six months she had watched as an entirely new side of Cameron Barnes emerged. As the owner of Dark Desires, one of the country's more prestigious kink clubs, Master C as he was known, had a reputation as one of the most hardline Doms around. She'd been equal parts terrified and mesmerized by him the entire time she'd been working at the club. But the ruthless man who often seemed to materialize out of thin air—*how could anyone move so quietly?*—which continually kept her looking over her shoulder, had faded quickly and been replaced by a far more likable version.

The only time she'd seen anything resembling the unyielding Dominant she'd known as Master C before Carl Phillips' arrival was a few days ago during their discussion about the ridiculous amount of money he was paying her as a nanny when she wasn't doing the work. He'd leaned back against his desk with his arms crossed over his muscular chest and his ankles crossed in a deceptively casual pose as he listened patiently and studied her intently. When she had finally paused, he'd pushed away from the desk standing to his full height before proceeding to explain in very colorful detail how much he would enjoy watching her Masters punish her for insolence if he heard another word about it. *Damnable man.*

He was awfully bossy for a man who was selling the club—just in case anyone was interested in her opinion—which of course they weren't. No, if Lara had learned one thing during her time at Dark Desires, it was Doms rarely asked anything even vaguely resembling permission after their initial negotiations with a submissive—they didn't need to, because they watched…everything.

"There's that enchanting Mona Lisa smile again. I'm wondering where your mind is wandering off to, precious girl." Peter's sweet words moved over the shell of her ear leaving behind heat far more intense than the warmth of his breath. They had all three been so exhausted by the time they'd returned to the penthouse each night the past week, they'd barely had the energy to shower before falling face first into bed. Obviously her body was beginning to protest the lack of attention because suddenly every cell felt as if it had been electrified. *Talk about being pathetic, holy craptastic, Lara, all the man did was whisper a question in your ear and your mind skips right to how fast you can get naked before you trip him and beat him to the floor.* Lara had big plans for Fischer and Peter after tonight's ceremony. She fully intended to have her wicked way with her Masters, even if it meant getting a few swats beforehand.

"My love, you know, even though I can't hear your thoughts clearly, it doesn't mean I'm not getting very strong emotions. Anytime we are skin to skin I'm gifted with awareness of what you are feeling, and right now I'm sensing you are feeling a bit neglected." She couldn't hold back her gasp of surprise, *damn it all to dirty dominos. How did he know?* When their grandmother had visited a few weeks earlier, the older woman had warned her as their bond grew, both men's abilities to "read her" would probably strengthen as well. But Lara had shrugged it off as something to worry about a few years into the future rather than just a couple of months. *Frack a big friggin' frog.*

Peter moved so quickly she barely had time to register the movement before she felt two heated swats on her thinly covered ass. The dress they'd chosen for her to wear was made of midnight blue silk and was the most comfortable thing she'd ever worn—except for the fact it was cut to her naval in the front and to the dimples at the top of her ass in the back. When she'd asked how she was supposed to keep her breasts from making a sudden appearance both men had simply shrugged. She was guessing they wouldn't be too happy about the double stick tape she'd used to secure the edges. Lara quickly banished those thoughts hoping Peter hadn't picked them up.

Gasping at the sting but immediately feeling her sex flood with moisture, Lara wanted to curse her traitorous body. Damn her horny self, it was going to give her away even though she wanted to act indignant about her stinging ass cheeks. Peter slid his hand up the back of her dress and Lara felt herself stiffen for just a moment. Before meeting the Weston brothers, she would have been mortified to have a man pawing her in plain view of others, but they had been slowing acclimating her to being naked in public. They'd teased her about being a prude, but she knew better. Even though they liked to remind her it was their decision when and if they displayed her in public, they had also been crystal clear about the fact they only shared with one another.

Peter's fingers slid over the slick folds of her newly waxed pussy lips and she heard him chuckle, *"Mi amōre, your body betrays you. Those little frown lines between your brows are trying to convince me you don't like to have your lovely ass warmed by my hand, but your juicy little pussy says something else entirely."* In her peripheral vision, Lara could see Fischer's all too arrogant smile. He knew exactly what his brother was doing to her and he obviously wasn't going to do a thing to distract him. "Which one do you think I'm more inclined to believe, precious girl?"

That was a rhetorical question, right? Because he surely couldn't be serious about requiring an answer when the truth was coating his fingers slick with her juices. *Fuck me, if he'd just push a little further forward and press just a smidgen harder...* "Brother, I do believe our sub is in need of a good orgasm. Those breathy little moans of hers are starting to attract attention." Lara felt as if someone had thrown a bucket of cold water on her, every one of her muscles stiffened and her eyes went instantly wide as embarrassment rocked her.

Fischer stepped in front of her and tipped her chin up with his fingers trying to gain her attention, but she was frantically searching to see who was watching them finger her to the edge of release in front of God and everybody. Lara hadn't even realized she wasn't breathing until his voice broke through her panic, "Stop, Lara. Look at me—and only at me. Breathe with me, baby." She gasped in the first breath as if she'd just run a marathon. "There's a good girl. Damn, sweetheart, I thought we were past this."

Chapter Two

Peter had been blindsided by Lara's reaction to his comment. Hell, there wasn't anyone even close to them, but her entire body had locked down when she thought she'd attracted attention by responding to his touch. The woman's body was pure fucking blonde bombshell perfection, but her parents' emphasis on modesty had definitely left its mark on her subconscious. She was just under five and a half feet tall with luscious curves and long blond hair falling in soft curls that always made her look like she'd just tumbled out of bed reminding Peter of a stereotypical Hollywood starlet from the fifties.

If he had to guess, Peter would assume her parents had encouraged the young beauty to hide her assets so she wouldn't draw unwanted attention. As a former Special Forces operative, he'd been in most of the areas of the world where she'd lived and knew all too well how dangerous they could be for a beautiful woman—particularly one whose golden hair and fair complexion would have made her stand out no matter what she'd been wearing.

It was damned frustrating to have to guess what was going through her mind. Even though he was finally beginning to read her emotions, he still couldn't grasp her thoughts and it was crazy-making. He and Fischer had wondered many times during the past couple of months how their friends managed to keep their woman happy when they didn't have the vaguest idea what they wanted. Kent and Kyle West had laughed out loud about their complaints, claiming they didn't need to be empaths because Tobi's face and body told them everything they needed to know. Kyle had actually shuddered, "It scares me to think about hearing what's going on in her pretty head because most of the time I think she is plotting our painful demise."

Gracie's husbands, Micah Drake and Jax McDonald, had been more circumspect. Micah had simply pointed out one of the things that made a woman so appealing was her mystique, Jax had agreed and then simply laughed while telling them to suck it up. Oddly enough, it had been Taz Ledek, who was, without question, the most dangerous of their former teammates, who'd provided the most valuable insight. Taz's Native American grandmother was a well-respected healer and Taz had obviously inherited some of her unique gifts. He'd asked if they were listening with their hearts or their minds, and Peter had been too stunned to even attempt to answer. When neither he nor his brother responded, Taz had simply nodded as if he'd done his part and leaned back in his chair casually continuing to sip his beer.

Looking back, Peter could see he and Fischer had both been trying so hard to sort through what she was saying, they hadn't been listening nearly enough to what she wasn't saying. She had adamantly denied the way she'd been raised had influenced her fear of public nudity, but Peter and Fischer both disagreed even though they hadn't taken the time to fully explore the issue with her yet. Her parents might have been trying to protect their young daughter, but the truth of the message had been skewed in the process. Public nudity would continue to be an issue until she understood her safety was in their very capable hands.

Returning his attention to the woman in front of him, Peter realized Fischer had talked her down fairly quickly, and that fact alone indicated they were making progress. Hell, the first time she'd panicked it had taken them over an hour to get her settled. They needed to work harder to identify the triggers so they could begin helping her overcome them. Neither he nor his brother were particularly committed to public scenes, but knew they could be fun on occasion. They wanted to help Lara reach a point where it was at least an option. Kyle had mentioned they'd had some of the same issues with Tobi, which surprised Peter because the woman was practically an exhibitionist now. Damn, maybe he and Fischer needed to speak with the Wests and see if they had any suggestions on how to help her find herself as a submissive.

When he finally withdrew his hand from under her skirt, he palmed her ass and gave the taunt little globes each a firm squeeze. "Precious girl, we're going to be discussing this later—count on it. But for now, let's join our friends and offer our congratulations, shall we?"

Her breathy, "Yes, Sir," would have been music to his ears if it hadn't been followed by a gasp of surprise. Fischer had still been pressed close to her and his frown let Peter know they had a new problem.

LARA HAD COMPLETELY forgotten about the phone in her pocket until she felt it vibrate against her hip. *Fuckalistic. Maybe with just a little of luck—* Before she'd even finished the thought Fischer moved around to stand in front of her, his eyes had narrowed and his entire expression immediately darkened. He leaned down and whispered against her ear, "Cupcake, that just cost you ten. You know the rules—you bring any electronic device into the club and you answer for it immediately."

A flash of warmth moved over her chest before moving up to paint her cheeks in a wave of heat she was sure meant her face was probably glowing scarlet. She silently cursed her pale coloring, even with make-up she'd never been able to hide the evidence of her embarrassment. Fischer's expression softened marginally, but the smile he gave her looked positively sinister. "Of course, since my brother and I are the generous types, we might be willing to negotiate, since this technically isn't a club function."

Oh, she could definitely take this ball and run with it. Even though she was trying to control her outward responses, her blood was surging to her nipples and sex so quickly she wondered if she wouldn't get light-headed. *Oh yeah, dropping into a dead faint won't draw any attention at all, Lara, you dope.* Hoping to distract him, she took a deep breath and spoke quickly, "That's right, this is a wedding—it just happens to be hosted here because the Barnes own the building. So those rules don't really apply. I needed my phone in case the caterers or someone else needed additional information…you know, for deliveries and the like." It probably would have been more effective if she hadn't been bouncing on the balls of her feet and babbling like a hopped up Energizer Bunny.

"Well, technically that is no longer true, precious girl. The paperwork was all finalized this morning. You now work for Kent and Kyle West, and I can tell you their rules about phones are every bit as strict as Cam's. I saw Tobi get a paddling that I am quite sure—even though she's had many—she still remembers vividly for having her phone in her pocket as she walked through the club. Hell, the club wasn't even open at the time, so as you can see, you are in quite a pickle here." Peter's words might have been those of a sexual Dominant, but his voice was sex set to sound. God the man had a voice that probably had girls dropping their panties all over the city.

Peter's hand was caressing her ass again, giving it a firm squeeze every few passes and Lara felt her entire body shudder in response to his touch. She couldn't decide if it was anxiety or anticipation—hell, it was probably a toss-up at this point. "Oh, I do so love having my hands on your ass—those lovely rounded cheeks fit my palm as if they were made for me. And seeing that creamy perfection draped over my lap makes it almost impossible to think because all my blood rushes to my cock." Dear God, they were going to make her come right there—from their words alone if she wasn't careful. When she tried to step to the side, Peter's palm slapped her ass with enough sting to make her gasp in surprise. "Don't you dare move, you are already in enough trouble as it is. You'd do well to listen to what your other Master has to say, *mi amōre*."

Well, I'm probably not in too deep if he's still calling me his love. She could hear her own heart beating a staccato pace and knew her breathing had quickly become dangerously shallow and much too fast. When Fischer looked down at her, his expression was considering and she knew exactly what he was seeing. Her nipples were already rasping against her dress, the fabric that had felt silky smooth just minutes earlier was now abrading the sensitive nubs. When he started to slide his hand in the front of her dress, she knew her situation was about to get a lot more dicey.

When the fabric didn't slide open, she felt him tense and she wasn't able to hold back her muttered curse.

FISCHER WAS BATTLING an epic internal battle to keep from laughing out loud. Lara was in so deep and he knew she had to feel like everything was falling down all around her. He wasn't sure how a sub who always seemed to make every effort to behave managed to consistently get herself in so much trouble. And the look of abject horror on her face when she'd cursed aloud had been almost hysterical. Their older brother, Adam, had complained endlessly about his wife's ability to distract him during scenes with her irreverent behavior, and Fischer was just now beginning to understand his frustration. Hell, Lara had a fucking phone on her, she'd taped her dress down to avoid flashing her lovely breasts—something he and Peter had been looking forward to enjoying, and now she'd spit out a string of curse words that would make every sailor in the room proud.

'I swear if she makes me laugh I'm going to paddle her sweet ass right here and now. Did you know she used double-stick tape on the front of her dress?'

'Nope, but can't say I'm terribly surprised, she was worried about falling out of it before we left the office. Now I know why she went up there.' Fischer could hear the laughter in his brother's tone and knew he was likely working to keep a straight face as well.

Lara Emmons was, without a doubt, one of the most submissive women Fischer had ever met, there hadn't been any doubt about that fact from the first moment he'd laid eyes on the little beauty. But her desire to *please* others seemed to get her into an inordinate amount of trouble and he'd be willing to bet she'd seen the tape as a way to please them by looking appropriate during the wedding.

'Jesus, Joseph, and Mary, she is racking up so many swats she isn't going to be able to sit for a fucking week. I'm not sure what to do with her.' Fischer agreed with his brother's assessment, but he didn't want to deal with the situation during the reception.

'We'll deal with it when we get back upstairs. I think it might do our sweet subbie some good to sweat it out for a while.'

TOBI WEST NUDGED her friend and nodded toward the other side of the room, "Gracie, check it out. I'd recognize that body language at a thousand paces."

Gracie's unladylike snort of laughter earned her a glare from Tobi before she spoke, "No doubt about that girlfriend." Tobi almost cringed as she watched Lara's face turn bright red, "Damn that girl needs to learn how to control her blushing, it gives her away every time. I don't know what she's done, but I'll bet you dollars to donuts she was trying to do the right thing and it backfired on her. That happens to me all the time."

This time, Gracie actually spewed punch all over the bar. "Damn it, Tobi." Tobi tried to give her friend her most sincere look of innocence, but when Gracie rolled her eyes, she'd known it was a wash. "Don't even try that with me, Tobi West. I know you far too well. If you've ever gotten into trouble because you were trying to do the right thing it was purely coincidental."

"I agree—and it's one of the things I love about her." Lilly West stepped up beside Tobi, giving her a quick hug before using her thumb to indicate the place where Peter, Fischer, and Lara were standing, "What's going on over there? And how the hell is she keeping her knockers from falling out of that dress? Damn I wish I was built like that, she really does have an amazing rack."

This time is was Tobi's turn to spit and sputter, "Holy shit, I can't believe you just said that." Gracie had stopped mopping up her mess on the bar to stare at Lilly with open-mouthed shock. "See? You even shocked Gracie, who knew that was still possible. Hell, I thought I'd broken her of that a long time ago."

Lilly looked around, no doubt making sure she wouldn't be overheard, before whispering, "Sorry, I'm just pissy because my men are holding out on me. My blood pressure was a bit elevated when I had my checkup—have I ever mentioned how much I hate it when Doms think they should be in the room during a sub's physical? Well, anyway this is a prime example of why that sucks. How was I supposed to claim everything had gone perfectly when they were in the fucking exam room with me? Damn it all to hell, I need to shoot something. I'm sure that would lower my blood pressure and several people here actually deserve it. Like that guy over there, did you see the way he was treating the woman he's with before Kent had a chat with him? I could shoot him and no one would care. I'd probably be up for some award in no time at all." By this time Tobi and Gracie had both turned to stare at the woman they considered their friend. The fact she was Tobi's mother-in-law was something Tobi considered one of her greatest blessings.

"How high was your blood pressure? It must have been really elevated if your men are withholding sex—and that really sucks by the way. And do your sons know about this?

And don't be telling me it's a secret either, you know I'll just end up in trouble with everybody if I try to keep something quiet. Really, I'm good at keeping secrets…usually. But damn if it doesn't always get me into trouble." Tobi's husbands were almost as protective of their mother as they were of her, and Lilly's husbands might appear laid back where their spirited wife was concerned, but they certainly weren't above reining her in on a very short leash when they thought her health or safety were being compromised.

Lilly's gaze never left Lara and the Westons', but her hand waved as if she were dismissing the question, "Oh, it wasn't that high…men are just alarmists sometimes. And I'm telling you, not getting any is certainly not helping the situation—nope, not helping at all. What do you think she did? Boy, they are sure having to work hard at looking pissed. I know that look—I get that a lot." By this time Gracie was laughing so hard she had tears running down her tanned cheeks and Tobi was quickly losing her own battle to keep a straight face.

"Damn, you change subjects faster than I do, and that's saying a lot. I don't know what she did, but knowing Miss Goodie Two Shoes, it couldn't have been anything too serious. I swear that girl's parents have scarred her for life. Living with missionaries in BFE probably instills a special level of *good* in people that I didn't get living in the seventh level of hell." Lilly turned and enfolded Tobi in a tight hug without saying a word.

"Kitten? What's going on? Are you alright?" The concern in Kyle's voice was easy to hear and as soon as Lilly released her, she found herself being pressed protectively against his chest. "If you're worrying about Lara, don't. I've known Peter Weston for a long time, and I can tell you he isn't really angry—he's obviously frustrated with their sub, but it's nothing every Dom in the room can't relate to."

Tobi wasn't sure why she was surprised he'd picked up on her concern for Lara because both of her husbands always seemed to know exactly what she was thinking. One of the many things she'd learned about Doms was their attention to detail—the way they studied their submissive was downright frightening at times. She and Gracie had joked one afternoon during a high-octane tequila-fueled pool party that they were a couple of orgasms away from having stalkers. The alcohol had clearly fogged their judgment, because they had both forgotten every square inch of the Prairie Winds Club—both inside and out, was closely monitored. The place would probably give the CIA and KGB headquarters a run for their money. Oh yeah, that had come back to haunt them, big time. *Damn it all to dangling daffodils, orgasm denial ought to be illegal.*

"We're fine. I just felt like hugging my daughter-in-law, that's all. No crime in that, is there? And if I can't shoot anybody, then I'll just hug people at random until I feel better. And you all will just have to cope." With that, Lilly stalked off leaving her son gaping after her in stunned silence.

"What the hell was that about?" Kent's voice sounded from the side, but Kyle just stared after his mom, his mouth still hanging open in shock. It was finally just too much and Tobi joined Gracie, as their nearly hysterical giggles filled the room.

BY THE TIME Peter and Fischer escorted her to where their friends were already celebrating, Lara was about ready to faint. She hated being in trouble—she always had. But hearing Tobi's and Gracie's giggling had provided the perfect distraction, she felt herself relax as she took what felt like her first deep breath since she'd stepped between her two Masters several minutes earlier. The men had stepped to the side shaking their heads as if women were the most confusing creatures on the planet, and Lara was more than happy to join her friends. By the time Tobi and Gracie had finished recounting Lilly's outrageous behavior, Lara had been laughing so hard she'd had to retrieve a napkin from the bar to dry her eyes.

She'd never lived in one place long enough to form any real friendships while growing up, so she'd been completely unprepared for all the shifting social dynamics of the world of teenage girls when she'd started pubic school as a freshman. It wasn't until she'd met the two women standing beside her that Lara had really started to understand the joy of being surrounded by good friends.

Tobi and Gracie winced when Lara told them what had taken place on the other side of the room. "Oh, girlfriend, you are in for it." Unconsciously rubbing her ass, Tobi shook her head, "I know from experience that cell phones are a cardinal sin…and just FYI, the same is true of iPads, anything with a camera is gonna get your ass in a pickle…or strapped to a spanking bench. Hell hath no fury like a Dom with a legitimate complaint."

"Yeah, not the brightest crayon in the box this one," Gracie added, using her thumb to indicate Tobi, "she thought she could cut through the club with her iPad on, but even though she was working on an order for the Forum shops, Master Micah's cameras don't miss anything."

"Yep, the rat-fink sent the video clip to both Kyle and

Kent. Damn those Doms stick together like glue. Anyway, I'd already lost my cell phone for a month, and damned if they didn't take my iPad for two months." The gleam in Tobi's eyes told Lara there was more to the story, so she just waited. "But I got even with them. I went shopping with Lilly." Evidently Lara's puzzled expression was enough to prompt another round of giggles.

Gracie leaned close and whispered, "When Lilly found out what her sons had done, she intentionally *misplaced* her phone about five minutes into their shopping trip. They were gone all day and no one could contact them."

"Of course, we'd forgotten about our bracelets." Lara knew the three women had specially designed jewelry with small tracking devices as an added layer of security. Tobi sighed and shook her head. "Boy I'm telling you, when the four of them stalked through Jezebel, everybody, and I do mean every single person in that restaurant, stopped what they were doing and watched the show." Tobi shuddered and Lara found herself dying to hear the rest of the story, but something about the way Kyle West had just looked at her from across the room set off all her internal alarms. Tobi and Gracie both followed her gaze, and Lara heard Tobi's whispered, "Oh no, I wonder what's happened. I know that look…and it never heralds good news."

Lara watched as the men conversed among themselves. Several pulled out their phones and spoke animatedly, their gazes flickering in her direction. But it was Peter's and Fischer's expressions that worried her the most, their eyes held something between worry and sympathy, and it was the most terrifying thing she'd ever seen. Lara felt Tobi and Gracie flank her, their arms going around her protectively as she started trembling so hard she wondered if she would shake apart.

The sound of her own heartbeat pounded so loudly in her ears it nearly drowned out the harsh sound of her gasping for breath. Lara saw both Peter and Fischer turn at the same moment to look at her as if they'd heard her mind racing as worry assailed her. For the first time, Lara understood the fear her grandparents must have lived with every time a stranger appeared on their front porch. Their daughter and her family had been traipsing all over the world and she knew they had to have worried themselves sick. Good God, she really was losing it if she was thinking about people she hadn't seen in almost a decade. Frantically reaching for her phone, Lara realized it was no longer in her pocket. Why hadn't she answered it or at least checked it? Anyone who would have called her was already in the room—everyone but those few people who'd been given her number as an emergency number for her parents. The horrible realization that washed over her made her knees buckle, and the last thing she remembered was the sound of chaos surrounding her.

Chapter Three

Kyle West had been his team leader when they'd both been Navy SEALs, so their connection was strong enough that Peter had known almost immediately the nature of the phone call his friend had taken. Hell, it wouldn't have taken a close friend or empath to read the man's body language. Kyle had gone on point the minute he'd looked at the screen on his phone and his clipped speech was a throwback to their time in the military. Ending the call, Kyle turned and started giving orders to members of his team who had gathered around. Peter saw Fischer pull Lara's phone from his own pocket and wince at whatever he saw on the screen.

Listening to Kyle recount his conversation with one of his contacts at the State Department sent a spike of fear through him. Peter wanted to put his fist through the closest wall when Kyle explained why the State Dept. had become involved and that Lara's parents were missing. The part of the world where they'd last been seen was anything but friendly to any humanitarian workers, and particularly unsafe for Americans who were considered a threat no matter how noble their reasons were for being there.

As if that news wasn't unpleasant enough, in his opinion the situation went from dire to straight up FUBAR when Kyle told them the case was being transferred to the Department of Homeland Security. *Yep, the entire evening was officially fucked up beyond all recognition.*

Letting his gaze flick to where Kent West stood with his phone pressed to his ear and his teeth clenched while he listened to whoever was on the other end of the line didn't do anything to reassure him that Kent was hearing anything more encouraging. Peter wondered if the other man's teeth would shatter from the pressure his jaw was exerting, hell, everything about his body language screamed anger and frustration. "Please tell me your brother isn't talking to Roberts. Goddammit, Lara doesn't deserve this."

'We need to get over there, Lara has obviously already sensed something is wrong and she'll know it involves her because of the phone call.'

'Agreed, I've never known anyone to call her that wasn't already here tonight.' Fischer's words might have been spoken in Peter's mind, but they hit him like a physical blow. It was true, in all the time they'd spent together he'd never known her to receive a single phone call from anyone they didn't know and that included her parents. *'Exactly. Have you ever known Mama Weston to go a week, let alone several months go by, without talking to us—all three of us?'* Peter mentally rolled his eyes, hell, his mother had nearly driven his commanding officers insane with phone calls when he'd been on missions. Mama Weston hadn't ever grasped the concept of "need to know basis" that was for sure.

Once Peter and Fischer started walking toward Lara, Peter saw the stark fear in her eyes and cursed himself for not going to her earlier. It was obvious Tobi and Gracie were offering their support, but he doubted they'd be able to keep her on her feet if her legs gave out and judging from the way she was hyperventilating, that was a distinct possibility. They were within just a few feet when he saw her knees start to fold out from under her. Both Tobi and Gracie shouted for help a split second too late and all three women crumpled to the floor in a heap of tangled arms and legs.

Kent and Kyle's fathers had only been a few steps away and they had the women untangled and were moving Tobi and Gracie back so Peter and Fischer could check on Lara. "I'm sorry. We tried to keep her up, but she just went completely limp." He felt sorry for Tobi, she was obviously worried for her friend. Tobi West might drive her husbands to distraction, but she had a heart of pure gold and every bit as big as the state she called home.

Kyle had pulled Tobi into his arms while Kent checked her over, Jax did the same for Gracie as Micah's hands skimmed over the voluptuous dark-haired beauty. When he discretely kissed her softly rounded belly, Peter knew they'd be sharing the good news soon. Peter looked up at Tobi and smiled, "You did a great job." And then looking at Gracie he added, "You slowed down her fall and that probably prevented her from being injured, and we're very grateful. Did she say anything before she fainted?" The women quickly related what had happened and by the time they'd settled Lara on one of the long sofas, her eyes were fluttering open. It was easy to see the moment she realized what had happened because her face flushed a brilliant crimson.

FISCHER PULLED LARA onto his lap as everyone gathered chairs around to discuss the disappearance of Lara's parents. He was barely keying in on his brother's participation in the conversation, but it was obvious the Wests' team was planning to send a team to find Lawrence and Rita Emmons. Fischer hadn't been a soldier, he'd known better than to even try. Hell, just seeing the toll it had taken on Peter had been enough for him to steer clear. As an empath, prolonged exposure to extreme violence was brutally painful and he had simply not wanted to be a glutton for punishment, to use one of Mama Weston's favorite expressions.

Fischer's hand rubbed soothing circles over the small of Lara's back—he just couldn't seem to stop touching her, and he wasn't sure if it was for her comfort or his own. When he'd looked across the room to see her eyes widen as if she'd been desperately trying to see past the darkness and she battled to keep the darkness from encroaching, he'd felt his entire world shift. He'd known she was special—that she was the one he and his brother had hoped to find, but the realization of human frailty hit him hard and knowing he couldn't reach her before she sank to the floor had made him almost physically ill.

He'd spent months waiting for his brother to visit Dark Desires and meet the luscious beauty now seated on his lap. Months of seeing her almost every day, but not being able to touch her except in his fantasies—and Lord almighty there had been plenty of those. While it had been pure torture, it had also given him time to get to know her—time to form the bond of friendship he knew made their D/s relationship particularly strong because at least on a very basic level, she already trusted him.

Lara felt perfect cuddled against his chest, her head tucked beneath his chin. Peter sat next to him and Fischer could feel his brother struggling to divide his attention between the woman their hearts had claimed as their own and the plans being made to find out what happened to her parents. Fischer was content to let her listen as the Wests' team put together a strategy that seemed more like a way to fend off Eric Roberts than it did to investigate the disappearance of a couple of missionaries—or at least he hadn't minded her interest until he realized she was listening far too intently.

Shifting Lara on his lap so he could whisper in her ear, he cautioned, "Cupcake, don't even think about getting involved in this operation. You'll find yourself in more trouble than you can imagine—and very quickly." When she stiffened, he knew he'd hit it dead center. "Perhaps we'd better head upstairs, baby, it might be the only thing that keeps you from adding to the already impressive number of swats you've earned this evening." He slid his hand under the hem of her dress to slide his fingers through her soaking sex. When she stiffened against him and tried to close her legs, Fischer snarled, "Don't even think about denying your Master access to your body, subbie, unless you have a particular desire to find yourself laying over my lap with your ass bared to everyone present as I give you the paddling you so richly deserve." Feeling her emotional turmoil, Fischer simply waited, his hand caught between her thighs. He could have easily forced her to open her legs for him, but that wasn't what submission was about. This was a test of her ability to trust him—to trust that he had her best interest in mind—even when she wasn't thrilled with the way things were playing out. Would she put herself in his care or deny her true nature and push back against her deep need to submit?

LARA FELT LIKE her mind was splintering in a hundred different directions. A part of her wanted nothing more than to curl up in a ball and cry—she knew where her parents had been posted last and disappearing in that part of the world was usually a one-way ticket to nowhere. Another part of her wanted to hear the men's plans to investigate her mom and dad's disappearance because no one knew them better than their only daughter, and she fully intended to be involved in any attempts to find them. She felt a sudden rush of guilt as she wondered if she could have helped if she'd been there.

The biggest part of her wanted to lose herself in her Master's touch, to simply surrender to him and let him lead her to a place where her mind could float free from all the frightening possibilities clouding her thoughts at the moment. If she submitted to Fischer, she wouldn't have to worry about anything for a while—and letting go of all the anxiety and fear, even if it was only for a short time, sounded very appealing indeed.

It felt like her body made the decision for her, and the prospect of being able to shut down the fears quickly taking over had been more temptation than Lara was able to resist. She relaxed her legs and felt a fresh rush of moisture coat her slick sex as Fischer pressed his lips against her ear and cooed sweet words of approval. "Such a good girl, I'm proud of you for being brave. And I promise to still your troubled mind." He turned her face to his, sealing his lips over hers in a kiss that was nothing short of a statement of ownership. There was no prelude, just pure carnal desire clearly spoken in a universal language as old as time. His tongue swept in to duel with her own before staking its claim. Fischer's scent surrounded her and pulled her mind into the churning abyss that her body had already willingly plunged into headfirst.

Lara had been so distracted by Fischer's kiss, she hadn't realized he'd picked her up and had moved until he set her on her feet in front of the elevator. She was panting, trying desperately to pull in enough oxygen to get her bearings. How on earth did the man manage to completely scramble her brain with nothing more than his kiss? She felt her knees tremble and hoped like hell they wouldn't fold out from under her again. Watching the doors slide closed shutting out the sounds of the main room, Lara looked over at Fischer just in time to see him enter the code that would open the elevator's backdoor when they reached the floor where their private office suite looked out over the club's main room. She looked down where his hand encircled her upper arm and wondered for a moment if he was trying to keep her on her feet or prevent her escape. *As fucking if...*the only escape she was interested in is the one that would shut off the fear pounding between her ears like the beating drums of the jungle tribes of the Amazon. *Damn those always scared the crapola out of me.*

Fischer seemed to sense she was sliding out of the moment, he turned to her when the elevator started to move, and simply said, "Strip." The one word command set her entire body on fire. The heated rush that blew over her made tiny droplets of sweat bead up on her chest as desire flushed over her skin. With trembling fingers, Lara gathered the hem of her dress and began pulling it slowly over her head. Since he'd already removed the tape she used to secure the dress's plunging neckline, it slid off easily.

She placed the silky garment in his waiting hand and shuddered as the air conditioning blew over her heated skin causing goose flesh to work its way across her bare breasts like ripples over water. The contrasting sensations sent her libido into overdrive and she heard herself moan softy as his fingers trailed down the side of her cheek to trace a line along her chin before continuing down the side of her neck. When he reached her collarbone, Fischer's finger rotated just enough so the manicured nail rasped down the outside curve of her breast. That simple touch felt like a line of fire and she gasped, her mind was already starting to spin as she struggled to process all the sensations.

He hadn't even touched the nipple, but it tightened quickly in response—as if begging him to linger and give it the attention it was seeking. "Your body craves a Master's touch, baby." *Only yours. Yours and Master Peter's.* She'd never responded to another Dom the way she did to the two of them.

Lara wanted to keep them for her own, but they'd only eluded to making their relationship more permanent at some point in the future, and she was determined she wouldn't beg—at least not for *that*. Okay, so maybe she was being old-fashioned, but it just "shouldn't be done" as her mother always said. "Good girls don't have to chase after men. Men may play with the bad girls, but they chase and keep good girls, Lara—don't forget that." She could still hear her mother's words ringing in her ears. When she realized she might never get another chance to hear her mother's voice, Lara felt her arousal fade as sadness moved over her.

Blinking back the tears that were threatening to fall, Lara realized the elevator door stood open, but Fischer wasn't moving—he was simply studying her, his gaze laser sharp. "What were you thinking about, baby? And don't you dare edit, I'm fairly sure your pretty ass is already going to be worn out before we've finished, and I'd hate to see you add to your troubles." His voice might have been soft, but the demand was easy to hear. The problem was, how much could she share without revealing how insecure she was actually feeling?

When she didn't answer right away, he sighed in frustration and hit a button on the small elevator's control panel that kept the doors from closing. He stepped to the side and pressed a small recessed button she'd never noticed before. Two toeholds emerged from the floor and a series of what looked like gold towel bars at various heights slid into position from a panel along the sidewall of the elevator. Turning to her he simply said, "Remove your shoes." She felt her body respond, but when she saw the hard look in his eyes, she took an involuntary step back. Fischer didn't say anything, he simply leaned back in a deceptively casual pose, crossing one ankle in front of the other and hooking his thumbs just inside the front pockets of his slacks. She studied him as well, there wasn't anything threatening in his body language, simply raw desire and steely determination. Lara took a deep breath hoping it would infuse her with the courage she was suddenly lacking as she slowly unbuckled the ankle straps of her stiletto sandals. Bending down, she picked them up and then held them out to him.

FISCHER WASN'T SURE a woman's simple act of trust had ever affected him more. He'd seen the indecision in her eyes and had practically been able to feel how torn she'd been downstairs. He would bet his inheritance the shock had been wearing off and she'd already started feeling guilty—playing every possible scenario over in her mind and always coming back to the *erroneous* conclusion that if she'd been with her parents this wouldn't have happened. And even though he wanted nothing more than to pull her into his arms and comfort her, that wasn't what she *needed*. Right now the beautifully bare submissive standing in front of him needed to be reminded that she was right where she belonged. She needed to know he and his brother would protect her even when it conflicted with what she thought she wanted. And she needed to feel the safety in consistency, and that meant holding her accountable for her behavior and following through on the punishment she'd earned.

Fischer had learned a lot during the time he'd worked for Cameron Barnes, the man might not have Fischer's ability to hear the thoughts of those around him, but Cam was the most intuitive Dom Fischer had ever met. The man known as Master C had taken Fischer under his wing and mentored him, teaching him that there were times the words moving through someone's mind were often little more than self-talk and therefore not entirely reliable measures of their true feelings. Recognizing the difference between what someone told themselves they should want and what their body craved was the difference between meeting the submissive's needs and just fucking—the difference between pushing a sub's boundaries to broaden their horizons and simply achieving the satisfaction of having power over another person.

Stepping forward to take the shoes from her trembling fingers, Fischer wrapped his hand over hers, holding her hand and her gaze for several seconds before speaking. "Do you trust me, baby? Do you trust me to give you exactly what you *need*?" He'd deliberately emphasized the word need, because he had no intention of giving her what she wanted—no, this was all about what she needed to still the turmoil he could see quickly overwhelming her. In that moment, Fischer had never been more grateful for the time Cam had spent tutoring him because every nuance of Lara's body language was practically shouting her need and Cam had taught him how to recognize all the signals. Taking her dress had exposed her physically, but he'd known taking her shoes would make her feel a whole new level of vulnerability—it was part of the reason subs were rarely allowed to wear shoes in the club.

Lara's sky-blue eyes filled with tears, but she didn't let them fall. Fischer watched her fight to pull herself out of the mental fog she was battling just enough to put on a brave face. "Yes, Sir, I trust you." So brave, but so fragile at the same time. Was it any wonder she enthralled him? Everything about her drew him in—and it had since the moment she'd walked through the front door of the club looking like the innocent she'd been.

"Thank you, pet. I intend to honor your trust by reminding you that a good Dom always keeps his word. If I didn't punish you as I told you I would, your mind would process that inconsistency and abstract it to any number of other circumstances. I want you to know—to know without question—all the way to the depths of your soul, that both Peter and I will always keep our promises." Looping the straps of her shoes over the end of the handrail where he'd hung her dress at the back of the elevator car, he turned back to her with deliberately measured movements. He wanted to give her mind time to process everything that was happening. Ordinarily, Lara's mind processed information at a pace worthy of a Mensa member, but this evening her thoughts were bogged down by all the emotional turbulence of her parents' disappearance.

It was his job to push all the disquiet aside, giving her mind and body the break it needed. The success or failure of the next half hour depended in equal parts on her ability to put herself fully in his care, and his ability to push her just enough past her usual boundaries to clear out the emotional sludge weighing her down.

"Slide your feet into the toeholds. Perfect, now lean forward and grab this bar." He'd chosen a bar low enough so she'd be forced to push her ass out, displaying it beautifully as if it were lifting and reaching for the strokes he planned to give her. But the toeholds weren't adjustable and she was a petite little thing, so her sex was going to be very exposed and those sensitive tissues definitely couldn't take the lashes his leather belt would lay across her ass so his placement was going to have to be very precise.

Lara wasn't a pain slut, so this would certainly be a punishment, but he knew it was going to take a lot to get her out of her head. It was going to be a delicate balancing act—skating on the edge between giving her enough to push her where she needed to go, and steering clear of anything extreme enough to destroy the trust they'd already built.

Chapter Four

THE FUCKING ELEVATOR was locked and that could only mean one thing. Peter took off for the stairs at a dead run, he was going to kick Fischer's ass for taking off with Lara before he'd finished with his team. And if his little brother was fucking their sub in the elevator, he was going to be doubly pissed because his cock was so hard he was sure he could use it to pound nails and running up the stairs with a hard-on was torture. Watching Fischer play with her downstairs had almost made him come in his pants and he hadn't done that since he'd been old enough to drive for fuck's sake. Reaching out mentally, he asked, *'Where the hell are you?'*

His brother's answer confirmed they were in the elevator, but Peter was unprepared for the scene he found when he rounded the corner to peer into the small space. Seeing Lara naked, her small bare feet shoved into toeholds and gripping one of several bars he hadn't even known were there brought him up short. But it was the red stripes across her upturned ass that had him freezing in his tracks. *'What the fuck are you doing? This is too much.'*

'No, it's not. It's exactly what she needed. Stay quiet and watch her—really watch her.' Peter wanted nothing more than to cram his fist in his brother's smug face, but he also knew if they intended to make this work long term they would have to work together and that meant appearing to

have a united front. Any differences in opinion would have to be resolved out of Lara's presence. She was much too perceptive and would be able to use any disagreements between them to her advantage—even if she didn't do it consciously, it would still happen. Peter had seen subs play Doms against one another all too often.

By the time Fischer finished with Lara's punishment and ordered her to kneel on the floor, she was sobbing and babbling about how sorry she was to have disappointed them. When he started to move to her Fischer stopped him with just a look. Peter didn't know what his brother was planning, but it was obvious he didn't think their scene was over yet.

Sobs racked her petite frame and Peter had to clench his hands into tight fists to keep from reaching down and pulling her into his arms. When she finally calmed enough to hear Fischer's words, he asked, "Tell us the rest, cupcake. You have to trust your Masters not only with your pleasure, but also with your pain, and most of all with your fears." Peter heard the hitch in her breathing and watched as her tear stained face tilted up, her gaze moving between them. Even with eyes swollen from crying and her tiny upturned nose bright red, she was the most beautiful woman he'd ever seen. But he held himself back, staying completely still because he knew she was watching—waiting to see if there was any indecision between them. And in an instant he knew exactly what Fischer had been trying to give her. His brother had known what their sweet sub had needed to purge the emotions she had been trying so valiantly to hold inside downstairs.

Seeing their united front, she deflated as if someone had stuck a pin in a balloon. Sagging, her shoulders curving in, she gave in again to hiccupping sobs, but these were entirely different. Through her gasps Peter barely heard her words, "I'm so scared they're dead. I should have been there. I was always the one to warn them when trouble was brewing because I'd hear the rumors first. I was small and everybody discounted me because of that. They thought I didn't speak their language because I didn't go to their schools so they spoke freely in front of me. I should have gone back. I was supposed to go back when I graduated. But I didn't…I…I was too busy having fun."

Peter was relieved when Fischer leaned down and scooped Lara into his arms. *'Grab her things and push the recessed button to the left of the control panel before you release the doors. If our members find those little features the damned elevator will be stopped all the time.'* Peter didn't doubt that—hell, it was a perk he hadn't even known about until today, and now he was more than a little curious what other secrets Dark Desires might hold. But for now, his focus needed to remain on Lara—she was going to need their support, and he had a strong suspicion they were going to need to watch her like hawks lest she decide to investigate her parents' disappearance on her own.

After sending the elevator on its way, Peter stepped into the office and watched as the wall panel that hid the steel door slid closed, smiling at the way it virtually disappeared into the wall. Yes, he really did need to talk with Fischer about what other secrets Dark Desires held. Turning his attention to the open door at the other side of the office, Peter listened as Fischer spoke softly to Lara, trying to soothe her by assuring her that she'd done exactly as he'd asked, and praising her for venting her frustration because it wasn't healthy to bottle those negative emotions up inside. "Sweetheart, Peter and I are honored that you trusted us enough to tell us your fears. It makes me sad that your sweet ass had to pay such a hefty price to get your mind to let go. I don't know who taught you that whole 'suck it up and handle it alone' mentality, but I'd sure like to point out the error of their ways to them."

Peter smiled at Fischer's words. Yeah, he'd like to be in on that 'come to Jesus meeting', too. He couldn't help wonder if her parents had ever allowed Lara to be a child. From what he'd learned, she'd been born in a small village where her parents were working at the time and she had essentially been raised by nursemaids until she was old enough to begin school. He'd wondered more than once how a couple of missionaries had been able to afford the household help, but had chalked it up to the destitute financial conditions plaguing the nations they'd lived in.

Her mother and father had homeschooled Lara, beginning her studies when she'd only been three years old. But by all accounts they'd only overseen her education, she was for the most part self-taught from what he'd been able to ascertain. And when he'd looked through her background information and seen what all she'd accomplished since returning to the U.S., he'd been amazed. He had to admit, he agreed with the notes Cam had made in her file that she needed to focus her efforts in a more linear direction—racking up numerous bachelor's degrees didn't really make much sense. Perhaps diverting her attention back to her education would help keep her from making a play to join the investigation of her parents' disappearance? They needed to find something to distract her. Peter agreed with the rest of the team—something was off about the whole situation, but none of them had known exactly what was tripping their internal alarms.

Discovering Homeland Security was involved had definitely been a game changer. Lara probably hadn't considered the implications of that piece of the puzzle. If she'd even been listening close enough she would have surely figured it out though because none of them had done anything to disguise their frustration. But since Fischer had been playing with her at the time, Peter seriously doubted she'd heard much of what was being said. Damn his brother had been having fun, Peter had seen it in his eyes—hell, he'd practically been able to feel Lara's sweet syrup sliding through his own fingers when he'd connected to Fischer. Peter's concentration hadn't been for shit, so he'd deliberately blocked their connection because he really had needed to concentrate on the impromptu sit-rep the Wests had called.

When Peter stepped into the hidden bedroom Cameron Barnes had built just off his office, he was pleased to see the contractors had finished the updates Fischer had initiated after they'd taken the helm at Dark Desires. Cam's preference for "stark" in his personal areas hadn't appealed to Peter or Fischer. He might give Fischer a ration of shit about his interest in aesthetics, but damn if his younger brother didn't have a real gift for making their surroundings perfect. Fischer had described the apartment Lara had been living in as a hovel, and the men Cam had hired to move her into his penthouse when he'd hired her as a nanny, had been even less charitable in their descriptions. It wasn't because she didn't have good taste, it had been all about economics, and Fischer had been thrilled to have her input on the redecorating project.

Peter had understood she was a college student and even though he had opted to live at home while attending college, he'd had enough friends that he understood students' sub-standard living conditions were par for the course. But he'd read the background work Cam had done on Lara, and he wondered how grandparents with a net worth to rival the assets of many small nations could allow their only granddaughter to live in an area so rough the local police steered clear after dark. Peter and Fischer had planned to ask her about her relationship with her family, but had been waiting until after the Barnes' wedding, all the planning had drained their time and energy. But now, it looked like they would be having that conversation sooner rather than later.

FISCHER UNDERSTOOD THAT for him personally, being a Dom was more than a sexual lifestyle choice, he'd always viewed it as the foundation of his personality. All of his interactions with other people were affected in some way by his Dominant persona. He'd seen the way people reacted to his physical appearance and he'd be lying if he said he hadn't used it far too often, but his air of authority was what had the more lasting impact. Physical attraction was overcome quickly if a person was an ass. But he'd recognized early in life that most of the people he met were naturally attracted to power. The allure of an authoritative personality was almost magnetic under the right circumstances—hell, he'd watched in amusement as Cam demonstrated the point in the checkout line at the local supermarket one afternoon. They'd been discussing the topic while driving back to the club and his boss had simply pulled into the parking lot of a grocery outlet store, smiled and said, "Watch and learn."

Cam's influence on Fischer as a sexual Dominant couldn't be overemphasized. Fischer was wise enough to know some of the things Cam had taught him served more as behaviors to avoid rather than practices to follow. His former boss had reminded him more than once he should never discount the value of a bad example. Cameron Barnes was one of the most self-aware people Fischer had ever met; Cam had claimed it was one of his most valuable assets and it was one Fischer strived to achieve. And right now he was painfully aware of the fact his cock was about to burst from the pressure of wanting to sink into Lara's sweet heat.

By the time he'd calmed her enough that he knew she was actually hearing his words, he leaned down and brushed his lips softly over her ear, "You did so well, baby. I can't begin to tell you how proud I am of the way you took your punishment. More importantly I'm humbled and honored that you trusted us enough to be honest about your fears. I meant what I said, cupcake—we don't just want the good, that wouldn't be fair to you or to us."

Peter sat down on the small table facing the sofa where Fischer held Lara and took one of her small hands, holding it between his much larger ones. Fischer watched in amusement as Peter seemed stunned for a few seconds at how tiny her hand was compared to his own. *'She is petite, and vulnerable right now—but at her core, she really is remarkably strong.'* Anyone else would have probably missed Peter's quick nod, but Fisher understood his brother almost imperceptible gesture of agreement. "We want the woman who submits so beautifully. The one who entrusts her body to us, knowing we'll give her everything she needs. But we also want the woman who needs to be held all evening because she had a trying day or because she's worried about someone she cares about. We want the woman who knows she can express her opinions without fear of the consequences—as long as she does so respectfully. Most of all we want the woman you are here." Peter placed one of his palms flat over Lara's heart and Fischer saw tear tracks down her blotchy cheeks again. Damn, she was going to be dehydrated at this rate.

Fischer nodded to Peter who then stood and held out his hand for Lara. They moved her into the attached bathroom and into the shower quickly. They hadn't tackled the remodeling of the bath yet, so it was still woefully inadequate in Fischer's opinion. He'd never been a big fan of minimalistic décor and this small room was next on his list for a makeover. The stark contrast of black accents against the bare white floors, fixtures, and walls was almost a shock to his senses after the much softer tones they'd used in the bedroom. As he and Peter set records for getting out of their clothing, he shook his head, "This room makes my eyes hurt. Let's get our girl clean and get the hell out of here." The soft snicker he heard from behind the glass shower door was about the sweetest thing he'd ever heard. *'Damn, I love hearing her laugh.'*

'I agree, and it occurs to me that we don't hear it nearly often enough.' Fischer agreed, but he wasn't entirely sure how to fix it—but he did know who to ask, and he made a mental note to call Tobi West first thing in the morning.

Chapter Five

Tobi West paced the length of the living room of the suite they'd rented. Even though it was a beautiful place to stay while they were staying in Houston, she was antsy and bored—a dangerous combination for her. "Will you please sit still? You're making me a nervous wreck. And your pacing is about to make me dizzy—if I throw up again, Jax and Micah are going to pack me off to the doctor—*again*. And I'll hold you personally responsible." Gracie was lounging back on the large sofa so surrounded by the pillowed cushions, Tobi wondered how her friend planned to get up without help if she had to make a fast trip to the powder room.

"Close your eyes and don't watch if you can't take it. And don't think for a minute I'm taking the rap for your husbands being anal…that's just a Dom thing—they were like that before I met them." Hell, every Dom Tobi knew was all tough-talking-macho-man until he found the right sub and then they all seemed to turn into mother hens almost overnight. But in Gracie's case, Jax and Micah's concerns were well founded, Tobi's best friend had struggled throughout her first pregnancy so everyone was worried this time around might bring the same challenges. Their mutual OBs had threatened to hospitalize Gracie more than once if things didn't improve the first time, and both of her husbands had been beside themselves with worry since discovering she was pregnant again. Both Tobi and her mother-in-law, Lilly, had spent a lot of time at the McDonald-Drake house making sure Gracie stayed in bed whenever Jax and Micah both had to be away from home during her first pregnancy—and would likely do the same this time around.

"It won't matter, I'll still be able to feel the wind whipping around the room. Good God Gertie, knock it off. When you are walking so fast I can feel the air moving and it makes me…oh shit—help me up…quick!" Tobi looked over and just as she'd figured, her friend was windmilling all four limbs trying to roll out of the plush pillows.

"Oh duck it." Tobi hurried to Gracie's side pulling her quickly to her feet. "Holy hell's bells and cottontails, you are sorta green there, girlfriend." Most of her words had been spoken to Gracie's back as she sprinted down the hall to the closest power room.

"Good save, kitten." Kyle's deep voice sounded right behind her and she squealed in surprise as she spun around slapping at his chest.

"Damn it all to donuts, you scared me. I swear you do that just for shits…umm, szitsus and giggles." Well crap, she probably hadn't covered that last curse quickly enough, but he'd nearly scared her to death.

"Oh, and you were so close." Kent's teasing voice sounded behind Kyle, she should have known they'd be together since they were working out of the suite. "Where's Gracie?"

"Ummm, she's in the powder room. She'll be back in a few minutes. Where are Jax and Micah?" When they stepped side by side, and crossed their arms over their chests without answering, Tobi babbled on, "I was just curious. I don't need them or anything. I just wondered if they happen to be around." Damn her rambling, it always gave her away.

"You know, brother, if I was the suspicious type I'd think our sweet wife was lying through her teeth." Kyle might have been talking to Kent, but his eyes never left her.

"Yeah, I would too, or at the very least I'd think she was not telling us something we probably ought to know." Damn, she hated it when they did this. Unless Lilly was around it was always two against one and sometimes that just made her dig her heels in deeper. Not that it was ever a good plan, but there it was—sometimes she just wanted to go down fighting.

She didn't answer other than to cross her arms over her own chest, keeping them low enough to raise her breasts, making them strain toward the revealing neckline of her shirt. She wanted to tempt them enough to shift their focus—and *there it was*. She wanted to do a happy dance when both of their gazes dropped to her chest, their eyes dilating, she was sure she'd gotten the distraction she'd been hoping for. Tobi knew exactly what they were seeing because the loose shirt she was wearing over her shorts was almost indecently low cut and without even glancing down, she knew the lacy bra she was wearing wasn't hiding anything from their view. "I know what you're doing, kitten. And unless you want us to take you up on that offer right here in the living room—where any member of our team could enter without warning, you might want to rethink your strategy."

"God, I hope she doesn't." Kent's words were a reverent whisper that sounded more like a prayer than a real comment. Damn, the two of them were forces of nature when they wanted to be, and as much as she hated to admit defeat, she slowly lowered her arms to her sides. Kent's soft curse was negated by the mischievous grin on his face.

"Such a good girl. Now, tell us what's up with Gracie that has you skittering like you've just been caught with your pretty little paws in the cookie jar." When Kyle poured on the charm it practically oozed out every pore. Damn his voice was enough to make her panties wet and from the unholy gleam in his eyes, he knew exactly what he was doing to her.

Since she couldn't think of a good reason to get a paddling for not blabbing, she said, "She didn't seem to be feeling well." She paused and realizing she'd dropped her gaze to the floor—*shit-shit-shit*—she looked to up see them both studying her like she was some sort of science experiment. "What?"

Kyle let out a sigh she recognized as his 'I'm almost out of patience with you' sound and grabbed her wrist pulling her close. It didn't escape her attention that his fingers were right over her pulse point. "Now, let me tell you what I see. I see a beautiful young woman who for some damnable reason still thinks she can lie by omission to the two men who know her delectable little body far better than she does. Your breathing is faster than it was a minute ago and that's saying something since I'd startled you enough to have you spitting out your faux curses. Your eyes are constricting, your chest is flushing, and your pulse is speeding up with every beat of your heart." He paused for a few seconds for effect and then simply said, "Talk."

"Geez, alright already, keep your hair on. Dang, you're gonna have a stroke if you don't lighten up a little." Neither of them seemed amused and over their shoulders she could see that Jax and Micah had entered the room, they glanced around for their wife and then zeroed in on her. *Fuck a fat fairy, sorry, Gracie, but I'm throwing your sweet toosh under the bus.* "Gracie is in the powder room because she's throwing up—again." Jax and Micah both cursed and took off down the hall, and Tobi felt like a slug.

Kyle's fingers came under her chin and lifted so her eyes met his. "Now, that wasn't so hard, was it? Love, that was important information for her Masters to have, don't you think? Part of the problem Gracie had during her last pregnancy was because she'd gotten terribly run down before Jax or Micah knew how sick she was. If they can get ahead of it this time, hopefully she'll fare better." Well drown him, when he said it like that it made perfect sense, even if she knew Gracie was going to read her the riot act for selling her out.

"Yeah, I know. It just seems wrong because it really isn't my story to tell, you know?" Tobi and Gracie had been friends and neighbors before she met the West twins, and they'd been through some pretty scary things together over the years. Hell, they were closer than many sisters Tobi knew, so tattling on Gracie just didn't seem right.

"Come on, let's see if we can't make a snack that will help settle her stomach when she comes back out. We ought to be able to come up with something." They moved to the kitchen and Tobi noted that Kent placed a phone on the bar before pulling out a tall stool and lifting her up onto the seat. Both men were always quick to help her up onto anything higher than a normal chair, they'd seen her grace in action too many times to trust her to manage alone. *I swear I'm going to be tall and overflowing with willowy grace in my next life. Oh, and model thin…with great teeth…and hair…well, hell. I need to start a list.*

WHILE HE PREPARED a snack for Gracie, Kyle watched Tobi and wondered why she seemed out of sorts. She'd been edgy since her conversation with Lara yesterday and he wasn't sure why, unless she was simply worrying for her friend. She and Gracie had been so wrapped up in planning yesterday's festivities, he'd wondered if there wouldn't be a letdown period when it was all over—so maybe that was the issue. Deciding to let her know what they needed from her might at least get a conversation started, but as usual she beat him to the punch. "Whose phone is that?" Tobi had pointed to the phone Kent had set on the counter in front of them.

Kent grinned at her, "Lara's" was the only thing his brother said, the rat bastard was obviously going to play with their wife and risk pissing her off. They needed her on board with their plan in case Lara got the call Eric Roberts was convinced was coming.

"Okay, I'll bite, but just so you know…I'm aware you are baiting me. Why do you still have Lara's phone?" Any other day Kyle might consider paddling her lush ass for copping an attitude, but he intended to let it slide today since she actually had a valid point, and they probably deserved to be called on it.

By the time he and Kent finished explaining their concerns and those of the representatives from the various government agencies they'd been consulting with, Tobi was twisting her fingers together and her brow was creased with concern. She didn't say anything for several minutes, Kyle and Kent just sat quietly letting her process everything they'd said. One of the things they loved about Tobi was the fact she was smart as a whip as their dads liked to say. She rarely rushed into decisions, contrary to what most people would have guessed, and she was actually very methodical when considering a problem and liked to gather as much information as possible before making a call one way or another. She might be impulsive in her personal behavior, but anytime they'd asked her to make a decision she'd looked at all the angles before making a call.

"So basically, everybody thinks the parents have either gone into hiding for whatever reason, or they're already dead. And if they are dead, then it's because of something Lara may or may not know." Damn, she'd given an amazingly accurate summation of several hours work—and she'd done it in two fucking sentences. Uncle Sam didn't know what he was missing and Kyle hoped Eric Roberts didn't figure it out.

Kent looked as stunned as Kyle felt but he managed to answer, "That pretty much covers it."

"Wonder if she really knows what they think she does? Because I can't see her failing to mention it before now. Lara is a straight shooter. I've never seen her do anything that made me think she wasn't being one hundred percent honest with me. But she is also pretty naïve sometimes, so I can see her not *realizing* she knows. Then again, maybe it's something they think she *has*, like a special decoder ring or something. Maybe some super-secret recipe for a food weapon—no that can't be right, I've heard the stories about her cooking disasters. Heckle and Jeckle she'd give me a run for my money on that front." Kyle was working hard to suppress his laughter because he knew Tobi had slipped from conversation to thinking out loud, but he let her continue because God knew he and Kent often got very valuable information while she narrated her thoughts.

More often than not it got her in trouble, but he didn't expect that to happen in this instance.

Watching her eyes clear, Kyle knew she'd come back to the moment and he couldn't help but smile down at her. "Kitten, I do love the way your mind works. I swear it's no wonder you and our mom are so close." *Analytical brilliance wrapped in beautiful soft silk.* He and Kent thanked their lucky stars every day their mom had met Tobi and sent her their way. They'd been avoiding Tobi's calls and emails for weeks because she'd been working for a local magazine and had wanted to do an article on The Prairie Winds Club, and they, on the other hand, hadn't wanted the publicity. But when Mama West put her foot down and insisted Kent arrange a meeting with the reporter she'd met during a visit to the magazine's office, they'd complied. From the first moment they'd met the pint-sized dynamo, they'd been grateful for their mother's insistence. And the fact the two most important women in their lives loved one another as if they really were mother and daughter was a huge bonus.

She grinned as if he'd just handed her the deed to the universe, "Thanks. I always take that as a compliment even though I'm not convinced it always is." Her grin was so infectious, Kyle couldn't help but chuckle and, he could see Kent's shoulders shaking with silent laughter as well. After a few seconds of silence, Tobi moved her thoughtful gaze between the two of them and said, "Okay, now I know there is more, so out with it." Damn, maybe she was spending *too much* time with their mom.

"Careful, sweetness. You don't want to let your mouth start writing checks your sweet little ass will have to cash later. I'd much rather fuck you than punish you." It always amazed Kyle that everybody thought Kent was the more easy-going of the two of them, when in fact he was far stricter. Kyle might talk more, but his twin was all about action.

"Sorry, Master." Kyle had to bite the inside of his cheek to keep from laughing because she was laying it on pretty thick, though he had to admit when she dipped her chin and looked up at him through her long lashes, it went straight to his cock. "I just want to know what it is the two of you aren't saying, because I know you, and it's there...I can feel it."

There wasn't going to be any arguing her point because she was dead on. But this time it was Kent who answered, "You're right, sweetness. We do need your help. We've kept Lara's phone because we're hoping to be able to backtrace any calls she may get about her parents. There are several things that don't add up, but no one wants to say anything to Lara just yet."

Kent had barely finished speaking when Tobi squealed and was literally bouncing up and down in her chair. "Oh, tell me what you want me to do—I'm going to be the best operative you've ever had, you just wait and see. Want me to ferret out information? I'm really good at asking nosey questions. Or maybe you want me to find out who her parents really work for...they might work for the CIA or something. Heck, maybe they were spying for Uncle Sam and got busted trying to steal top secret missile locations or vials of germ warfare stuff." Kyle looked at Kent to see the same horror reflected in his eyes that Kyle was feeling. How on earth had they lost any semblance of control over this conversation so quickly?

Obviously Tobi had noted their response, because without skipping so much as a beat, she added, "Maybe they know where Jimmy Hoffa is buried...yeah, that's probably it. You want I should find out, Boss? Huh? That what you want?" She'd ended with the corniest mafia gangster accent he'd ever heard and before they could even respond, raucous laugh sounded behind them and they turned to see Jax and Micah leaned back howling with laughter. Gracie stood between them, and even though she looked pale, her grin said she'd heard Tobi's outburst as well.

Kyle walked over to Gracie and wedged himself between Jax and his wife before grasping her elbow and leading her carefully over to the bar. Helping her up so she was seated beside Tobi, he slid the small plate of crackers and mild cheese he'd prepared for her over before moving to the refrigerator to get her a glass of milk. "Here you go, Gracie, hopefully this will help settle things down for you. I hated to see you stranded over there between those two laughing hyenas." She smiled and thanked him, but he noticed she only nibbled at the snack and even though neither of her husbands mentioned it, he knew they'd also noted she wasn't eating. They all settled into a relaxed conversation as they bantered back and forth about the best way to handle irreverent subs and he was grateful Gracie seemed to relax.

Jax took the lead explaining to Tobi what they had in mind when they'd asked her to answer Lara's phone. She seemed disappointed that they wanted her to simply listen as much as possible, and to follow any instructions they gave her during the call. They were all wearing earbuds and would be able to hear everything the caller said so they'd be able to coach her during the conversation. "Tobi, it's important you say as little as possible in case whoever is on the other end knows Lara well enough to realize you aren't her. We'll feed you questions so you won't have to worry about that. The thing I want you to focus on is keeping yourself in character, it's awfully easy to say 'she thinks' for example instead of 'I think'. A small slip-up like that can blow an entire operation."

Kyle was impressed with how attentively she'd listened to Jax's instructions and he was glad they'd decided it would be better to let someone besides he or Kent coach her. Too much would be riding on the call, which the alphabet agencies expected, so they needed Tobi to listen and follow orders, and everyone agreed it would probably be easier for Jax to impart the information. Hell, everybody knew how much the little imp liked to challenge both he and Kent, so handing the job over to Jax had been an easy call.

Just as they finished cleaning up and prepared to move into the suite's living room, Lara's phone lit up the word "Dad" and began playing "Papa was a Rolling Stone" by The Temptations. *God save me from subs with quirky senses of humor.* Micah took off running to the small room where they'd set up their computer equipment and Kyle nodded to Tobi, "You're up, kitten."

Chapter Six

Lara relaxed under the hot water as the shower rained down in muscle massaging pulses gently driving out the tension in her shoulders. Her ass was throbbing from the punishment Fischer had meted out earlier, damn he'd been tough on her and even though she wasn't thrilled with him, she understood what he'd been trying to do. Lara knew she tended to bottle up her fear and she'd felt herself locking up her emotions as soon as she'd heard her parents were missing. Shuttering her feelings was a habit she'd learned as a child—her parents had been relentless in the admonishments to show no fear and to hold her temper in check.

Being the only kid in the village with looks that didn't resemble anyone else's hadn't been easy. Her parents had drilled it into her from an early age the importance of not drawing attention to herself, so the 'pale-skinned kid with the light hair' wasn't considered a threat or worse yet—possessed. Every time her family moved into a new area, Lara was forced to hide until her dad could convince the local religious leaders that she wasn't some demon sent to destroy the integrity of the village and poison the minds of the other children.

As she'd matured, Lara had wondered more than once if her dad wasn't paying off the tribal chiefs to keep her off their radar, because even as inexperienced as she'd been, their leering looks hadn't been difficult to interpret. But it had been their sudden *in-the-middle-of-the-night* moves that had been the most suspicious. Her family had never kept many personal possessions—she hadn't been allowed to keep any more than she could pack in an hour. Her parents had insisted it was to avoid the heat of the day, which in most of the countries they'd lived in was a reasonable excuse—but their explanation had started to seem less and less *reasonable* as time wore on.

Leaning forward to press her forehead against the cool tile, Lara's mind drifted back to the night her one and only boyfriend had walked away from her. She'd dated Simon Ericson for several weeks before joining Dark Desires, and he'd seemed more interested in her background than her future. She'd met him late one afternoon after stopping at an outdoor café for a cup of coffee. While she'd been walking home from class, Lara had been almost overwhelmed with the strange feeling she was being watched as she'd made her way down the tree-lined street. She'd stepped into the small shop to place her order and then moved out to sit on the patio hoping she could figure out what was going on.

She'd almost finished her coffee when a young man sat down next to her and smiled as he pushed another cup of her favorite latte in front of her. At her questioning look he'd simply said, "I asked the barista" and shrugged as if that was all the answer needed. Lara looked at the barista who grinned and gave her a thumb's up. They'd started talking and before long she realized time had gotten away from her and it was getting late. When he'd seen her nervously glancing at her watch, Simon offered to give her a ride home. She'd hesitated—all those safety seminars her freshman year in college had evidently made at least a small impression, and he'd praised her for being cautious. He'd shown her his college identification card and a driver's license with an address not far from where she lived and for whatever reason that had seemed like enough reason to trust him. Later she'd wondered why it had made her feel safer—something she still didn't understand.

Lara had been dating Simon for several weeks when he suddenly announced he was moving to Washington D.C. and essentially disappeared from her life. He hadn't called or even emailed her after moving. It was if he'd simply ceased to exist, vanishing into thin air. The entire time they'd dated they had rarely gone out in public together, Simon always insisted he enjoyed her company and didn't see any reason to share their time together with anyone else. He had never wanted his picture taken, but she had managed to snap one candid shot with her phone, which had mysteriously vanished from her phone not long after he'd moved. Their "dates" had almost always been walks along the beach or at small hole-in-the-wall places that rarely had more than a few other customers.

Since she'd never had a boyfriend, Lara hadn't realized how strange the whole thing had been until after it had ended. When she'd mentioned it casually to a few of her friends one evening during a study session, they instantly expressed their concern. None of her friends had ever heard of him, and when she'd described him, they'd all sworn they'd never seen anyone matching his description on campus either.

One of her study partners worked in the Registrar's Office and had offered to check on him, as it turned out Simon Ericson had never been a student at any of the University of Houston campuses. Lara hadn't understood why he'd bothered with fake identification, but her friends hadn't been shy about expressing their opinions—and none of them were particularly comforting.

Simon had never pressed her for sex and there had been times when she'd practically begged him for it. After several rejections she had finally quit asking, the humiliation still burned despite her friends' assurance that there wasn't anything wrong with her. Looking back, she had to admit he'd seemed more interested in hearing about her life before moving to the U.S. than he'd ever been with what she'd been doing recently. He'd told her small anecdotes about his family and friends, but never enough that she had felt as if she'd really gotten to know him.

Lara took a deep breath trying to bring her thoughts back to the present when she heard the shower door open. She shook off the melancholy thinking about Simon inevitably brought on and turned to see Fischer watching her as if he was seeing her for the first time. It really should be illegal for any man to be so gorgeous. He had the face of an angel and Lara had watched women at Dark Desires literally walk into walls because they'd been staring at him. "What were you thinking about, cupcake?" His voice was soft—pure seduction, but there was no question he was going to demand an answer.

Straightening, Lara turned to fully face him, but couldn't seem to make herself meet his intensive gaze. "I was thinking about how strange my life is sometimes. How little I really know about dealing with people. I guess I started out thinking about my parents and just kept jumping from point to point until I was lost in the memory of how I was fooled by a man I met during college."

Fischer stepped into the shower with her, and prompted her to continue while he washed and conditioned her hair. "Tell me about him. You've never mentioned this before." He was right, she and Fischer had talked a lot during their frequent lunches together at the club's deli where she worked, but she'd never mentioned Simon because, quite frankly, she'd been embarrassed to admit how naïve and easily taken in she'd been. Just as she started telling the story, Peter stepped into the shower. He didn't say anything, just smiled and nodded for her to continue.

There were times when their ability to speak to one another telepathically was just plain creepy. It was obvious Peter hadn't needed to ask what they were talking about because he already knew. But Fischer's gentle touch kept her distracted enough that she divulged far more about her odd relationship with Simon than she had intended to. The tension in the small space was almost palatable by the time she'd finished telling them about her experience.

PETER HAD ENTERED the bathroom just as Fischer finished sending out his mental SOS. And listening to Lara's story about Simon Ericson didn't do a thing to allay his concerns for her parents, he was becoming more and more convinced they were more than simple missionaries. As a former Special Forces operative, Peter simply did not give any credence to coincidence. Ever.

Why would a man who simply wanted to pick-up a pretty coed need to pretend to be a student? And even then, most civilians wouldn't have the resources to be that well prepared. Oh, he could answer the question easily—to make sure his young, naïve mark felt safe enough to allow him to get close to her. Hell, the guy had clearly played Lara from the beginning. Most young women had been burned by guys often enough by the time they entered college that they were more than a little skeptical. But Lara's upbringing had been so unconventional she'd been easily duped. And while she might not be willing to admit it, he'd heard the insecurity that had subtly entered her tone as she'd spoken. She'd taken the guy's lack of interest in her physically as rejection. Personally, Peter wondered if the bastard hadn't been gay because it was almost impossible to imagine any straight man being able to resist the little blonde beauty. Hell, he and his brother wanted to fuck her all the time—and while he was grateful the man hadn't taken her, it was difficult to imagine how Ericson had dated her for several months and not enjoyed her delectable little body.

Peter watched her shoulders roll in and listened as her voice dropped as she spoke, all the while fighting the urge to slam his fist against the wall in frustration. Lara Emmons was one of the most beautiful women he'd ever met. She was a walking wet dream as well as being smart, funny, and sweet. Hell, if he and Fischer had designed their "perfect woman" you would have sworn they'd been describing Lara. His chief concern was the fact she hadn't really lived her life yet—he worried that if they moved too quickly, someday she'd realize how much she'd missed and want to reclaim a part of her missed youth. He'd seen it happen in his circle of friends and the resulting heartache had sent more than one of his friends into drunken tailspins.

Once they'd all dried off and moved into the bedroom, Peter pulled Lara into his arms and simply held her for several minutes. A part of him wanted to simply hold her close, but he knew there was a part of her that needed the reassurance that she was indeed desirable. He'd never met a woman yet who didn't suffer at least occasionally from the fear she "wasn't enough". If he and his brother had their way, Lara would never be plagued by that question again. Rubbing his hand in small, soothing circles over her lower back, Peter was pleased when she relaxed into his embrace.

He'd known from the beginning he would be playing catch-up in their relationship because she and Fischer already had a solid friendship. But he'd been pleasantly surprised at how quickly he and the little sub had bonded. He knew that her friendship with Tobi and Gracie probably played a large part in how easily she'd accepted the possibility of a ménage relationship. Seeing how happy her friends were in similar arrangements and knowing polyamorous marriages could work would have certainly helped calm any misgivings.

When he saw Fischer finish turning down the bed and move into position, Peter led Lara to the edge of the bed so she faced his brother. Fischer's eyes blazed with lust and Peter felt Lara's entire body begin to vibrate against him. Leaning down, he spoke softly against her ear, "Look at how much he wants you, *mi amōre*. We both want you more than you'll ever know. You are pure magic and it slays me that you don't know it." He pressed butterfly kisses from just below her ear skimming over her quickening pulse and following a line to the top of her shoulder. When he reached the tender spot where her neck and shoulder met, he opened his mouth and let his teeth graze the area they'd discovered was particularly responsive. He felt her shudder and wanted to smile. He looked up and gave Fischer a quick nod.

"Come here, baby. I want you to ride me. I can't wait to feel your hot little pussy wrapping my cock in your wet heat. You're so tight, squeezing me like the softest glove in the world. There ya go, slide right on down so I'm—holy fucking mother of all things sacred, when your pussy ripples around me I think I'm going to lose my mind from the pleasure." Peter tried to disconnect from his brother's emotions because he felt his own control skating far too close to the edge and damn it, he'd like to at least get inside her pretty little ass before he came.

Using the palm of his hand, he pressed gently between Lara's shoulder blades, lowering her down onto Fischer's chest. The surge of sensation he got from his brother was nothing short of pure bliss, as Fischer's mind registered the feeling of her tightly puckered nipples pressing against his chest and the soft sound of Lara's gasp as his chest hair raked over the sensitive nubs. Oh yeah, Fischer was struggling already and Peter knew he needed to get Lara's pretty rosette prepped and get inside her or he wasn't even going to get to ride in this rodeo.

"Pet, I'm going to get you ready to take us both, but I need you to help me out, okay?" Lara moaned and Peter couldn't hold back his smile. "Oh, precious girl, I do love that sound. But I need you to say the words, alright?" They hadn't taken her together often enough that he felt either of them knew her body well enough to assess how she was handling it. And until they did, he and Fischer would both need to double check to insure she was cognizant enough to use her safe words. And making her verbalize her desire was a sure way to keep the line of communication open.

"Yes, Sir. Please. Just—just tell me what you want me to do. I'm green…oh so green." Lara's use of the club's stop light system satisfied him that she was making an informed decision and he immediately dribbled a fine stream of warming lube at the top of her ass and watched it run in a slow stream over her pert little hole. Using the tip of his finger, he slowly massaged the lube into the flexing tissue surrounding her snug opening before pressing his finger just inside the tight ring of her anal sphincter.

Peter heard Lara's sharp intake of breath and when her body tightened around his finger he nearly came just from the anticipation alone. "Oh, sweet girl, I'm going to love pushing into your tight ass. You are going to milk me dry in no time at all. Hell, right now my goal is to get inside you before my balls spontaneously combust." And he hadn't been exaggerating. Feeling her rippling muscles trying to suck his finger in deeper and imagining how they were going to feel around his cock was maxing out his self-control in a big hurry.

By the time he'd worked a second finger inside, Lara was pushing back against him just like they'd taught her and Peter was trying very hard to tune out Fischer's running commentary playing out in his mind. Damn, he wished his brother would give it a rest already—he didn't have to share *everything*. There was no need to stack his pleasure telepathically while Peter was already trying to hold his own at bay. *'Knock it the fuck off or I'm gonna kick your ass, little brother.'*

'You can try.'

'Jesus, what are you five fucking years old?' They'd been replaying this same banter, under different circumstances since they had, in fact, been five and eight years old. Fuck, it was a wonder their mother wasn't bat-shit crazy having raised three boys who always knew what everyone was thinking. It hadn't surprised Peter or Fischer that their mother's response to finding out they couldn't "hear" Lara had been riotous laughter so out of control their dad had finally taken the phone from her to find out what was going on.

Peter leaned forward, running his palm up the length of Lara's spine from the peak of her rounded ass cheeks down into the valley shielding the small of her back and then back up the sloping incline until his hand spanned between her shoulder blades. "You are so beautiful, your pretty little hole is all soft and pink and ready for me. Hang on, pet, this is going to be a wild ride." He watched goose bumps race over her skin in anticipation of his possession, ordinarily he'd take time to admire each and every small nuance of her response because knowing their effect on her was intoxicating. But right now, he couldn't think past pushing into her and losing himself in her submission.

Pressing slowly inside, Peter was trying hard to shift his focus from the intoxicating feel of her ass opening for him as Lara arched her back and pushed back against him. "That's perfect, *mi amōre*. Keep pushing back, let me in, beautiful girl, and I'll take you on a magical ride." His breathing hitched as the widest flair of his corona slid past the outer ring of muscles and her pretty hole closed around his shaft. "Oh fuck me, sweetheart, you feel so amazing." He held still letting her adjust and giving himself a few seconds to reassemble his control. Hell, he wasn't sure how long he was going to be able savor the moment before his body demanded satisfaction, but for just a few seconds he wanted to simply enjoy the small ripples as she pulled him deeper.

He'd kept his palm flat against Lara's back, it was important to maintain the connection because that small demonstration of his dominance would reassure her that he was in control. It would also allow him to anticipate any movement, he was worried she might become so lost in her desire she'd suddenly surge back against him and injure the delicate tissues he was trying to gently stretch. "Just lie still and let us do all the work, precious girl. We don't want you to make any sudden movements and hurt yourself, do you understand? Give me a color, *mi amõre*."

Lara's soft groan was satisfying but not enough, the sharp slap to her already tender ass caused her to gasp before answering, "I'm green, Sir. Very, very green. And—oh crap on a coconut I know there was another question, but I really don't remember what it was. I just need for you to move—PLEASE." Peter knew he should make her answer, but his body was also demanding that he move.

"Hang on. Don't move or you'll get another spanking, and I'm not sure your beautiful red ass can take another punishment just yet." He felt her relax beneath his hand and when his eyes met his brother's over Lara's shoulder, he didn't need their telepathic link to know it was time.

Peter wasn't sure how they managed to keep their pace slow and measured as long as they did—alternating their withdrawals and thrusts so one of them was buried deep inside Lara at all times. He could feel her desire swamping him as if he was mainlining it, and his control finally snapped. *'Let's go. I can't wait any longer and I want you both to go with me.'*

'I'm right there with you and we'll take her over with us—she is close.'

They stayed in perfect sync even as the pace increased. Peter leaned down when he felt her ass tighten around his cock like a fist and growled against her ear, "Come now, *mi amõre*." Lara's response was immediate and cataclysmic. He felt the wave of muscle tension move up her spine beneath his hand a split second before she screamed. The muscles of her ass tightening rhythmically around his cock, the constriction was just this side of painful, and the bliss that followed sent his mind into a total whiteout. Hell, Peter didn't know how long his mind was off-line—his release had stolen everything—even his ability to breathe. Sucking in a big gulp of air, he hoped the infusion of oxygen would kick-start his brain back into gear. Jesus, Joseph, and Mary, he should probably be grateful his heart hadn't stopped beating.

Chapter Seven

Lara stared at the box sitting on Fischer's desk as if it were a snake coiled to strike. Her mind had shut down after hearing him tell her that the box had been delivered by a private courier who had claimed he had been paid in cash to bring the box to the club. Everything around her had become little more than muffled sounds the moment she'd registered the distinctive handwriting. As long as Lara could remember, she had envied her father's handwriting but had never been able to recreate the fluid artistry of his pen strokes. But now, staring at her name written across the top of the sealed box, she felt like she'd fallen into another realm. She could see everything was the same in her peripheral vision, but the sounds around her were muted as if they were traveling through water. Nothing existed but the box.

"Lara? Are you alright? Do you know who this is from?" Fischer's words finally broke through the fog, but only because he'd turned her so she was facing him, his large hands cupped over her shoulders and he'd given her just enough of a shake to startle her back to the present. She hated seeing the concern in his piercing green eyes and she wasn't sure her answers were going to do anything to allay his fears.

"Yes…well, yes the second question. I know who the box is from—or at least I know who addressed it." Well, it wasn't exactly addressed. Her name was written on the top and that was all, which seemed odd to her for some reason, but her mind didn't seem to be able to focus enough to worry about that just yet. "But in answer to your other question, I don't know if I'm alright yet." Fischer looked at her for several long seconds before pulling her against his chest and simply holding her close. She knew he couldn't hear her thoughts, but he was probably picking up the waves of uncertainty she knew must be surrounding her.

Lara had always hated making others worry about her and she sure seemed to be doing a bang up job of it since finding out her parents were missing. And now, here she stood staring at a brown cardboard box as if she expected aliens to pop out of it and whisk her off to some far-flung galaxy. When Fischer snorted a laugh, Lara looked up at him almost in a panic. She was going to melt into a puddle if he'd finally managed to hear her thoughts because they were usually focused on ways to get either him or Peter into bed. *Yep, all those years of being a good girl turned you into a nympho, Lara. I'm so sure your family will be thrilled with your fallen ways.*

FISCHER SENT OUT a mental call to Peter and knew his brother would come bursting in their office any minute, but his concern for Lara was growing by the second. He hadn't been overly concerned about the box until the courier had become evasive in his answers. The messenger was obviously nervous about being questioned, but it hadn't taken Fischer but a few seconds with the young man to know he was telling the truth. The kid was a student working part time at one of the restaurants Fischer frequented, so even though he didn't know the teen personally, he did recognize him—and the young man would have certainly recognized Fischer as well.

Questioning the messenger had been an exercise in frustration because the kid really didn't know who the man was who'd paid him to deliver the package. The young waiter had questioned the man about the contents because he'd worried about delivering something illegal but had been assured the small box only contained harmless personal items. The kid's physical description of the man who had paid him didn't match the one they had of Lara's father or grandfather, and Fischer had tapped into the kid's thoughts enough to *see* the man so he'd known the young man wasn't lying. If the Prairie Winds team was right and, the Emmons were operatives, they would certainly know how to disguise their appearance, all he'd be able to do was relay what he'd seen. His abilities often posed ethical dilemmas—how much information should be *taken* without the subject's consent? When did another person's right to privacy trump other people's need for information? Fischer had often struggled with these questions, but today had been a no-brainer, anything that kept Lara safe was fair game.

He'd watched as she looked down at the box and all the blood seemed to have drained out of her heart shaped face. She had completely checked out mentally—he hadn't needed any psychic skills to recognize *that* disconnected look. Damn, he'd had to gently shake her before her eyes had cleared and he'd known she was back with him. Whatever she'd seen had shaken her so badly he just pulled her close and held her until Peter burst into the room.

"What happened? Is she okay?" Peter's panic surprised Fischer—probably more than it did Lara, because he was accustomed to his brother responding to a crisis by going into what he and Adam teased their middle brother as being his 'soldier mode'. Peter had been the mediator when they'd been kids and that had carried over into his adult life. When he entered the military, he'd learned to block out the turmoil around him as best he could, and that required him to remain as emotionally level as possible. So seeing him so frightened on Lara's behalf was playing havoc with Fischer's own response simply because that sort of energy was very contagious.

Fischer explained about the delivery and then silently updated Peter on what he knew about the young man who'd shown up with the box. What he didn't know was why on earth Lara had checked out just by looking at her name written on the top of the box. "Baby, can you tell us what has you so upset when you haven't even opened the box yet?"

When she pulled back, Fischer felt the turmoil rolling off her as Peter pulled her into his arms. "Come on, *mi amõre*, tell us what this means. We can't help you unless we know who to kill." Fischer was grateful his brother had found a way to diffuse some of the tension and was relieved to see the corners of her lips turn up in a shy smile.

She finally pushed back, slowly disengaging herself from Peter's hold and stepping back. God he hated the way she was rubbing her hands up and down her slender arms as if she were cold. Taking her hand Fischer led her to the large window, he'd noticed when he first met her she would make an effort to stand in the sunshine at every opportunity. He'd assumed she'd become accustomed to the tropical climates where she'd grown up, and even though Houston wasn't exactly the North Pole, the temperatures could be erratic. She gave him a grateful smile and seemed to relax as the sun warmed her pale skin.

"I'm sorry I freaked out on you, but the handwriting on the box is my dad's and it threw me for a minute." Both he and Peter waited patiently for her to continue, it was easy to see she'd been thrown by the delivery. "I heard what you said about the messenger and that sort of surprises me because neither of my parents have ever sent me anything other than a post card or letter. And how did they know to send it here? And how did they get it to someone to even have it delivered? And if it's in my dad's writing, then I wonder if my mother knows he's sent it? I really don't know what to think about this."

Once she finally took a deep breath, Fischer nodded, "I'm sure I speak for Peter when I say we are wondering some of those same things. And if you don't mind, we'd like to get the Wests' team in here before you open it." She didn't voice any objections, just continued looking between them and the box. Peter slipped out of the office but Fischer could hear him speaking on the phone before the door leading to the hallway had even closed behind him. "Come on, let's go check out the back garden. I'm anxious to see how the landscaping is progressing and you can soak up some more sunshine."

The building that housed Dark Desires was u-shaped and the enclosed back area had always been little more than an eyesore before they decided to utilize the space. Before they'd erected the tall fence that now enclosed the rectangular space, they'd excavated the entire area and then brought in truckloads of topsoil. The landscape designer they'd hired was a Mistress at the club so she had thoroughly enjoyed incorporating small, secluded areas for scenes as well as a couple of more public areas for demonstrations. Hell, the bondage elements she'd incorporated alone were going to make the area popular. He was particularly proud of the netting over the top, it was virtually invisible to the naked eye during daytime hours, but at night it gave the impression of a star-filled night sky. Being able to see the stars in Houston was a rare treat because the lights of the city washed them from view. But the view would help enhance the feeling of isolation for couples who enjoyed the peace and solitude that was so hard to find in larger metropolitan areas. The net had the added benefit of enabling them to keep the area cooler during the hot Texas summers and it also kept it safe from drones with cameras.

Damn those things were becoming a real problem for their security team and an issue they'd need to address in the very near future. Dark Desires prided itself on being ultra-exclusive and a large part of that distinction was their guarantee of confidentiality. They militantly guarded their clientele's privacy, and no one wanted their picture taken entering a kink club.

Their membership list included wealthy businessmen who didn't need their reputations tarnished by narrow-minded hypocrites who would exploit their kinks. They also counted a number of politicians and religious leaders among their members and having their lifestyle choices splattered across the tabloids would destroy their reputations as well as the club's. Micah Drake had mentioned he was working on a signal that would scramble a drone's ability to navigate as well as electrically scramble any data they were trying to gather and Fischer was anxious to find out how that was progressing.

He and Lara talked about all the plans for the project and how much progress had been made as they walked through the area. They had been easing her into a position in the office and this was one of the first projects she'd been assigned. It was easy to see she was distracted, but Fischer was impressed with her ability to provide him with critical updates even when he knew her mind wasn't completely focused on their conversation. As they were inspecting the narrow walkways that had already been laid out using native stone, Fischer got a message from Kent letting him know they'd scanned the box and it was safe for him to bring Lara back in the building. She'd seen the text and gasped, "Safe? Scanned? They thought it might be a bomb or something? Holy crap, why would anyone think my dad would do that?"

He stopped and faced her, "Baby, someone could have imitated your father's handwriting just to fool you. You have to remember, we're always going to err on the side of the angels when it comes to you—your safety will always be first and foremost." Fischer didn't give her a chance to respond, taking her hand he led her quickly back up to the office.

PETER WAS RELIEVED when Lara appeared marginally more relaxed when she and Fischer returned to the office, even though she did seem surprised to see Kent and Kyle West as well as Jax McDonald and Micah Drake all waiting for her. Micah stepped forward and smiled at her, "Sweetness, the box appears to be clear, but if you don't mind I'd like to open it for you. I'll set the contents out for you to look over. Just in case someone has planted a surprise for you." When Lara nodded, Micah flashed her a big smile, "Such a good girl, perhaps we can get you to prevail upon Gracie and Tobi to follow your example."

A snort of laughter from the door let Peter know Tobi and Gracie had finally made their way to the office after making what the men had declared, "The Gracie Detour". He must have looked confused by their remarks because Jax had rolled his eyes and explained, "I swear that woman pees every twenty minutes, by the time the baby gets here she won't ever get out of the bathroom." When he'd looked over at Gracie she'd just grinned and shrugged.

Everyone looked on as Micah opened the box and began setting items on the desk for Lara to look at. There were only three things inside, which seemed odd considering the size of the box and the trouble someone had gone to making sure she'd received it. Lara's gasp when the Bible was set out surprised Peter, "Lara? Why does this surprise you?"

"My dad would not have sent this to me unless he knew he was in trouble—and even then I'm not sure he would have willingly parted with it. He kept it with him always and was continually making notes in the margins—it drove my mom to distraction. She swore someone was going to think he was plotting world domination he took so many notes about the places we lived." Peter glanced at his teammates and noted they'd obviously keyed in on the same question he had—why the hell would a missionary make so many notes about the people and places they were living? And the fact he'd done it in the margin of his Bible really set off Peter's alarms. The only plausible explanation was that Lara's dad was more than he'd appeared to be, and the worrisome part was that he'd evidently involved his daughter.

"What about this?" Micah held up a gold locket and Lara's eyes widened.

"Wow, I didn't even look at that. Seeing my dad's Bible

threw me. The locket is one my mom always wore, it was a gift from her mother. It had a small slip of paper inside with a note but I was never allowed to read it." Lara popped open the small piece of jewelry but the piece of paper that fell out didn't appear to be old to Peter. When she gently unfolded the scrap, she tilted her head and he saw small frown lines appear between her brows. "This isn't from my grandmother, this is also in my dad's handwriting."

"What does it say, cupcake?" Fischer had moved closer and Peter could feel the tension radiating off his younger brother. He might not have ever been in the military, but the need to be in control was just as firmly ingrained in him as it was each of the former Special Forces operatives in the room.

"It says, *'Seek direction from your heritage to find the common thread…Marilyn Monroe, the Beatles, Seals and Croft, James Bond, and Kiss. Feed at eleven.'* What on earth does that mean?" Lara seemed genuinely puzzled when everyone in the room smiled.

Kyle quickly got Carl Phillips on the phone and was reading the note to him while Peter explained, "Carl is a cryptologist. He works for the Prairie Winds' teams, and he's always our go-to guy for these things. I swear he's never met a puzzle he couldn't unravel."

When Kyle laughed and closed his phone, they all turned their attention to him, "Carl said if we can't figure this out we're a disgrace to music lovers everywhere and that we shouldn't be allowed to own radios or any number of other devices he named. He didn't seem too thrilled to be interrupted on his honeymoon, but since it was for Lara he was willing to tell me the answer." Everyone in the room laughed, but Lara who still looked confused by their irreverent behavior. "Anyway, he said the common thread is *diamonds* and that you should look for clues at the house you were raised in or at your grandparents' home, someplace where your 'heritage' would be. 'Feed at eleven' is evidently a bit trickier. But he said he doubted it meant the kitchen since it says *feed*. But he thought eleven would be a time or direction."

"Diamonds? How did he get diamonds out of—oh, wait, I know…song titles. Holy crap on a cactus he's amazing. Remind me to never play a trivia game with him." Peter knew the instant she realized the significance of what she'd just learned because he'd heard the small gasp and felt her stiffen beside him. "I need to get to my grandparents' house as quickly as possible, they might be in danger. And why would a couple of missionaries care about my grandmother's diamonds?"

'I'm convinced her parents weren't working only as missionaries—and I'm equally convinced Lara doesn't know what they were a part of.' Peter glanced over Lara's head at his brother who gave him an almost imperceptible nod.

Micah pushed the last item across the desk and looked at Lara expectantly. "What about this, sweetness. Any idea what this means?"

Lara picked up the faded photo of a small blonde girl on a rocking horse and smiled. "This is a picture of me. My grandfather bought me this rocking horse because my grandmother wouldn't let him take me riding on a real horse until I was five. I'd forgotten my mom had this picture or I would have asked for it."

"Do your grandparents still have horses?" Jax was leaning back against the credenza behind Fischer's desk and for the first time Peter noticed that his friend seemed to know Lara's family. When Lara looked confused, Jax added, "I know your grandparents, Lara. They are family friends but I haven't been to their estate for a long time. Do they still have the track and horses?"

Lara smiled, "I don't know for sure, but I'd be surprised if they'd gotten completely out of the horse business because my grandfather loved them. I don't think they are still active in those social circles any more, but I'm not really sure. I haven't seen them in a while, they had some sort of falling out with my parents. My mom also told me they weren't happy when I didn't want to use my trust fund for college." By the time she'd finished speaking she was once again looking down at the picture in her hands—stroking her finger lovingly along the surface.

Peter was struck once again by the fact her grandparents had so much money, yet she seemed to be perfectly content with so little. But now he had to wonder about his earlier harsh judgment of her grandparents, obviously they'd loved her as a child, and perhaps the separation hadn't been entirely their fault. Well, it looked like they'd be finding out soon enough.

The call Tobi had answered the other day hadn't done a thing to answer their questions, the man on the other end had simply said, "They'll want what was stolen from them—all of it. When you have secured the items call back on this number for further information and perhaps they'll make it back to you." They had definitely downplayed the last part when they'd explained the situation to Lara, but he was certain she'd seen through their best efforts to assure her that she wasn't responsible for making sure her parents emerged safely from whatever it was they'd gotten mixed up in. Peter suspected Lara's father was alerting her to something, but he wasn't sure what. He also agreed with the other members of the team, it was looking more and more like Rita Emmons was every bit as involved as her husband.

After making plans to visit her grandparents' estate north of Houston, the Masters of the Prairie Winds and Dark Desires decided it was time for a bit of fun distraction.

Chapter Eight

"Tell me again how we ended up in this pickle." Gracie looked expectantly at Tobi but Lara knew the Central American beauty didn't really expect an answer. She'd been so grateful Jax had agreed to make the arrangements for them to visit her grandparents, Lara hadn't cared much about the mess Tobi had gotten them involved in.

"Stop complaining, you know perfectly well all the Doms are going to go easy on you because you're knocked up. And that means Lara and I are going to get to deal with all the tricks they've got up their sleeves." Tobi shuddered before continuing, "Did I tell you all six of them raided the shops at the club? And they wouldn't let me see what they picked up, either. Well, except for these outfits. Damn it to daffodils I don't know how this happened. That bet should have been a sure thing."

Lara and Gracie both laughed, "Yeah, Gracie told me that you'd say that. And that you've said that same thing every time you have lost a bet."

"And I might add that every time she manages to pull me into one of her *sure things*, I end up naked in front of people doing something crazy. Make Tobi the Greek tell you about last Halloween." They were all three standing in front of the long marble counter in the master bedroom's dressing room in the West's suite putting the finishing touches on their hair and make-up before they reported to the kitchen. They were supposed to serve their Doms a seven-course dinner—of course the food had been catered in since the men all knew better than to allow any of them to cook. Kyle West had explained to his exasperated wife that the hotel had insisted he sign a sworn affidavit stating Tobi wouldn't be allowed to cook anywhere on the property after the fire department had been summoned not once, but three times during their last trip to Houston. Evidently it didn't matter they'd stayed at different hotels each time, word seemed to travel quickly between competitors when it came to pyromaniacs.

Lara turned to Tobi and raised a brow in question launching the other woman into a rant, "Oh drown me. I swear, Gracie, you have a stunted sense of adventure sometimes. Sure it was a little bit chilly by the time we were done, but we sure did get lots of treats. Of course our men got a few things we had to hide, but I've still got Snickers bars stashed and they haven't found all the *toys* they were given. Damn, I still can't believe the size of those butt plugs—you'd think doctors would have more mercy."

Gracie laughed, "She bet Kent she could go a whole week without cussing. I was going to bet with the men, but she pulled the BFF card on me and guilted me into buying a ticket for an all-expenses paid cruise on the Titanic." When Lara giggled Tobi glared at them both as Gracie continued, "Anyway, guess how long she lasted. Never mind, I'll tell you because this was a record, even for Miss Potty-Mouth over there."

This time Tobi's cheeks tinted pink with embarrassment as she shrugged, "How was I supposed to know it was a set-up? Damnable men. You should never trust twins by the way."

"Anyway, just as she seals the deal with Kent, Kyle grabs her from behind in one of the moves we'd been learning in our self-defense classes. That's another mess she got me into by the way." Looking over at Tobi, Lara almost laughed out loud at the ridiculously fake look of innocence she was struggling to maintain. Shaking her head, Gracie continued, "Tobi manages to actually take Kyle down, which shocked everybody, including her. But she also managed to let loose a string of curses worthy of a Guinness's record—four seconds flat."

"Hey, Drama Diva, we need to get to the kitchen, so I'm going to cut to the chase here." Turning to Lara, Tobi grinned, "We had to do strip Trick or Treating. Every stop cost us a piece of our costumes. You'd be surprised how quickly you end up naked even when you started out in full Marie Antoinette regalia." Using her thumb to indicated Gracie, Tobi laughed, "Catherine the Great over there didn't fare any better. But just seeing the looks on our Doms faces when we walked out in those elaborate costumes was worth all the effort."

"True, but we'll never get to pick out our own costumes again. Case in point these damned skimpy maid's outfits." All three of them looked down at the revealing outfits their Doms had given them before breaking out into fits of giggles.

Fischer watched the women walking down the hall and felt his blood rushing out of his head directly down to his cock—hell, he'd be lucky if he didn't pass out. The outfits he and the others had picked out barely covered them, but it didn't matter because they wouldn't be in them long anyway. Everyone involved—except Lara—knew tonight's fun had been planned to distract Lara from the emotional strain she'd been under since learning about her parents' disappearance. They planned to visit her grandparents' estate tomorrow, so tonight's fun would hopefully keep Lara from worrying about it.

Fischer had laughed out loud at the look on Tobi's face when they'd asked her to deliberately lose the bet. Even though he didn't know her well, it hadn't been difficult to figure out the bubbly little blonde wasn't accustomed to loosing on purpose. He'd been standing next to Kyle who had leaned close and whispered, "Tobi is compulsively competitive...this will be a good lesson for her." When Fischer didn't respond, he'd added, "Don't worry, she'll do it because Lara is her friend. She just has to get over the shock of it first." Kyle's chuckle let Fischer know he was enjoying his wife's discomfort—a lot. Fischer wasn't sure what Kent had whispered in his wife's ear, but she'd blushed a deep red before nodding her agreement.

As if it had been choreographed, each sub took her place between her two Doms standing quietly waiting for instructions. Fischer was thrilled Lara hadn't even hesitated to take her place between Peter and himself as they all stood in a casual circle talking. "Everything for dinner has been delivered and is in the kitchen ready to be served. One of the caterer's staff is waiting to show you where everything is, he'll leave before you begin serving." The Doms had been in agreement that no one but club members would be allowed in the suite during their "dinner party". A Dominant might love showing off his or her lovely submissive's body in the club or during private parties, but outside of the lifestyle they were almost always notoriously possessive. He'd heard submissives accuse their

Doms of being full-grown toddlers because of their *"Mine!"* mentality and it was probably a fairly accurate analogy.

Fischer was able to relax since he was only picking up random thoughts from around the room, over the years he'd become so accustomed to blocking whenever he was in a group setting he often did it without even realizing it. The fact he could hear the others clearly if he tried emphasized the fact he couldn't hear Lara—and it drove him crazy. The others were all playing their parts flawlessly, and even though he couldn't *hear* her, he could feel Lara's emotions, which were a nice mix of anxiety and anticipation. *Perfect.*

PETER PLACED HIS hand over the top slope of Lara's curvy ass and smiled at her soft gasp. She was listening intently as Jax and Kent explained the rules for dinner. *'I think our sweet sub needs some distraction. She's listening much too closely—hell, you know how she is, she will follow all the rules and where will be the fun in that?'*

"Totally agree with you, brother. Let's see if we can't derail her train of thought.'

Fischer ran his hand under the back of her skirt and when Peter felt her shift positions he knew his brother had instructed her to spread her legs for him. When he looked down at her, he was pleased to see her cheeks blushing beautifully and the flush of arousal beginning to spread across her chest. He could hardly wait to get her naked, he loved watching her ivory skin wash with pink and then rose as she became more and more aroused.

Tobi's voice broke through his thoughts when she asked, "So let me get this straight. We're supposed to serve you seven courses and we aren't allowed to talk to each other *and* we're competing against one another as well?"

"Sweetness, don't think of it as a competition, think of it as putting forth your best effort to please your Masters—avoiding the toy basket we've filled for you is just a bonus." The unholy gleam in Kent's eye sent a shiver down Tobi's spine that Peter could feel from across the room. He held back his laughter because Tobi seemed to be the only sub who was actually focusing on the instructions, which wasn't going to work out well for her since the three of them weren't allowed to talk to one another. Hell, that rule alone was going to get Tobi in a world of trouble because her natural inclination to help her friends meant she would definitely be talking.

'I'm betting Tobi is naked before the third course.' There was no way Peter was betting against him. Hell, his brother was probably being generous. Everyone who knew Tobi West liked her. There was an effervescence about the little imp that drew people to her. From what other members at Prairie Winds had told him, Tobi had blossomed under Kent and Kyle's care. She'd had a very rough childhood and had been living in survival mode for years, but she thrived on her husbands' ability to set boundaries even though she tested their ability to do so regularly.

After the women had gone into the kitchen to get their instructions from the caterer, Peter looked up at Kyle and laughed, "How long is your spirited sub going to stay dressed? Is there a pool going already?" The staff at Prairie Winds regularly bet on anything and everything with the proceeds going to the winner's charity of choice—and Tobi's antics were among their favorite wagers.

"No there isn't a need for a pool, she won't last long enough for us to set it up. Hell, why do you think we added the no talking rule?" They all chuckled as they made their way into the dining area. They'd extended the table so there was plenty of room between each of the six chairs in anticipation of their fun. When they weren't serving, their subs would either be kneeling on the large cushions between their Masters or more likely, they'd be laying over the edge of the table for one reason or another. Each pair of Doms had filled their own small wicker basket with toys chosen specifically for their sub. He and Fischer had picked out a vibrating butt plug, a tube of clit stimulating gel, nipple clamps, and a remote controlled egg vibe.

Peter was relieved when they finally sat down, walking around with the hard-on from hell tended to get old rather quickly. He'd seen his friends all adjusting themselves in their trousers as they settled into the thickly padded captain's chairs so at least he hadn't been alone. Looking across the table to where the Wests were seated, something in Kyle's drink caught his eye. When his friend picked up the drink, Peter realized the two round objects at the bottom of his ice-filled glass were faintly tinted glass Ben Wa balls—*sadistic bastard*.

God he was glad to see the caterer leave through the front door. The young man had been beet red as he'd been escorted out by Ben Monroe, a former Marine who was fairly new to the Prairie Winds team. They'd paid the delivery guy handsomely and the restaurant owner, who was a member of Dark Desires, had assured them the kid would keep quiet—from the look on his face he'd likely be too embarrassed to tell anyone about the crazy group and their scantily clad servers.

When Kyle got the nod from Ben that they were clear, he pulled a small remote from his pocket and the partition above the bar separating the dining area from the kitchen lifted slowly disappearing into the ceiling. Not to anyone's surprise, Tobi was chattering away as the subs loaded their small trays with crystal cups of shrimp cocktail. The knowing look in Kyle's eyes and Kent's chuckle was made even sweeter by Tobi's gasped, "Well, shit."

The women had been instructed to make a complete circle around the table before serving their Doms. And they'd been assigned either clockwise or counter clockwise rotations for each course—those assignments were posted on the refrigerator. Each Dom also had a copy of the list because no one doubted that as dinner progressed, the women would become less focused—thus giving the Doms additional opportunities to use all the goodies in their baskets. *Yes, indeed. Let the games begin.*

Chapter Nine

Tobi clearly should have thought this through more carefully. Hell, they hadn't even served up the first course and she'd already screwed up—*twice*. And her own ratfink Masters were going to make an example of her, she just knew it. She quickly double-checked the chart so she'd know which direction she was supposed to go and took off. She heard Gracie's muttered curse and knew she was right behind her, that left Lara standing in the middle of the kitchen looking at the chart as if she had no idea what it was for. Hell, Lara probably didn't know since her Masters had been totally distracting her during the instructions. It had been glaringly obvious they'd deliberately set her up because she was such a good girl—something Tobi was never accused of. By the time Lara finally set the small cups in front of Peter and Fischer she was trembling.

For once Tobi was grateful her Masters were not only pushy, they were also kind-hearted, and they spoke up taking the focus off the fact Lara's men were looking through their toy basket with exaggerated interest. "Kitten, do you know what you did wrong?" Kyle was enjoying this entirely too much, boy oh boy, had she ever walked into a mess of rattlesnakes when she'd agreed to this dinner party. She had to fight the urge to do the face-palm gesture at her own stupidity.

"Yes, Sir. I was talking and then I said something that

probably sounded like 'shit'." Well, it probably had because that was exactly what she'd said, but hey, it was worth a shot, right? When all six Doms laughed, she knew her ploy had just been blown out of the sky in flaming glory. *Damn it all to Dalmatians.*

"Good try, sweetness. But I'm afraid these are transgressions that cannot be ignored. What kind of example would we be setting as club owners if we let these pass?" *Oh brother, he's really laying it on thick. Hope I don't gag on all the PCBS.* One of the terms Tobi had introduced the club's staff too was politically correct bull shit, and her husbands had been none too pleased. When they'd complained, she had politely told them if they didn't want to be called on it, they shouldn't do it—boy had that ever been a mistake. She'd gotten a swat with a big wooden paddle from each of the Dungeon Masters later that evening and she suspected several had taken more than one turn—frick-frack, you couldn't trust anybody these days. Damn her ass had stung like a bitch for hours afterward even though she knew several of the men had pulled their swats going easier on her as the evening progressed.

Kent had turned her so he could tuck her skirt up in the back securing it over the waistband. *Well, hell. It's not like it was really covering me anyway.* "According to the rules, you only lose a piece of clothing if you are last to serve your Masters, so that honor is going to belong to Lara this round. But, we still intend to hold you accountable for talking and the word that sounded so much like shit—to everybody who heard it." The jackass actually had the nerve to make a joke at her bare butt's expense, she started thinking of all the ways she could get even but one glance at Fischer Weston stopped her cold. *Drown me, how did I forget about he and Peter's special gift.* When his eyebrow raised she just shook her head and he grinned.

Naturally, Kyle hadn't missed their non-verbal exchange, but rather than focusing on her, they both turned to Fischer. "Care to share, Master Fischer?"

"Well, since you asked. I do believe your lovely sub was plotting against you, and just for enforcing the rules, too. Tsk, tsk. Shameful. Really, it's just shameful."

It was too much. He'd probably flunked out of drama school for being corny. When both Fischer and Peter burst out laughing she felt her face heat until there wasn't any doubt about how red it was. *Damn and double damn.* This time Kent just shook his head and pressed his palm against the middle of her back to bend her over the edge of the table. "Just think, sweetness, you'll be the first one to make a mark on our paddle." Fuck a duck, she'd forgotten about the small wooden paddles laying at the top of each Dom's place setting. They'd had each of the subs' names engraved on them and then set black Sharpies to the side so for every swat a sub got, she was to make a tally mark behind her name.

Not that there was much question who was going to win this particular competition, but her men had promised her something truly spectacular if she "won". It didn't matter to her that they were protecting Gracie—because she's preggers and Lara—because, well that shell-shocked look on her face pretty well summed it up. Okay, and maybe "winning" was a bit misleading in this particular case, but none of that mattered to Tobi, nope—not at all, because a win was still a win.

Each of her husbands quickly gave her two solid swats with their damned paddles, but then they ran their fingers through her wet folds and knew exactly how turned on she was. They both chuckled and Kent had made sure she made the hash marks before he had her kneel on the cushion and began feeding her bits of shrimp cocktail. In the back of her mind, Tobi realized Gracie was already kneeling between Jax and Micah—they wouldn't have had her stand that long because she tended to lock her knees and invariably made herself lightheaded in the process. Glancing over, she noticed they weren't giving her sweet friend any of the spicy shrimp cocktail but they were feeding her some kind of small cracker with what looked like cream cheese spread over the top. When she'd helped make out the menu, Tobi hadn't even considered the first course wouldn't set well on Gracie's empty tummy. *Damn, some friend I am. Glad her men were paying better attention.*

"Princess, just in case you didn't hear all of the rules, since you were last serving your Masters, you owe us a piece of clothing and we've picked out something special for you from our little basket of toys." Peter knew Lara had heard him, but she had barely blinked, so he took a second to rub his hand up and down her arm a few times until he felt her focus zero in on him. "Good girl. Remember, we are observing the club's stoplight system for safe words tonight, but there shouldn't be anything to happen that you aren't fully capable of handling." At her quick nod of understanding, he continued, "Take off your shirt, *mi amõre*."

Lara's eyes widened and he saw the blush move over her cheeks, but she reached up with trembling fingers and began slipping the small pearl buttons free from their moorings. God in heaven he was proud of her, "Such a good girl. So brave. And it really would be a pity to keep these lovely tits of yours hidden." He knew she was still struggling with being naked in front of others, but this was a good opportunity for her to become a bit less self-conscious—not that they ever wanted her to be completely at ease being naked in public. After all, *that* would take away quite a bit of their fun.

The white cotton blouse of Lara's costume only had three buttons, but she'd only managed to free two of them when her hands started shaking so badly Peter gently pushed her fingers to the side and helped her. She actually seemed somewhat relieved when Fischer pulled it over her shoulders and let it slide slowly down her arms. They'd chosen a set of nipple clamps that would hold the small bells attached to the chains, but they were mild enough Lara would be able to wear them for a much longer period of time than any they'd used before. Using the ice cube he'd taken from his water glass, it didn't take Peter long at all to get her nipples tightly peaked for the clamps. "Those look beautiful, *mi amõre*. And I have to admit, I really love hearing the tinkling sounds the bells make. I'll be looking forward to you moving around the room with their soft sounds filling the air." He and Fischer settled her on the cushion before sharing their small dishes of shrimp cocktail with her. Peter had seen her sigh of relief when she knew she was below the other men's line of sight and didn't even try to hold back his smile. She was sure to feel better when she saw Tobi's skirt was still tucked in exposing her bare ass to everyone's view.

The chilled cucumber soup was served next and this time it was Gracie who was last because she'd walked the same direction as she had the first round instead of checking the list—which seemed odd for the normally detail-oriented woman. Peter watched as Micah unbuttoned her shirt, Gracie looked almost relieved. Jax laughed, "What's the matter, *cari mio*?"

Micah leaned forward circling his tongue around her nipple and Peter heard her sharp hiss. While they'd been ransacking the club's shops, Micah hadn't wanted nipple clamps for tonight's fun and games explaining Gracie's pregnancy made her much too sensitive for anything but the lightest nipple play. Peter raised an eyebrow at Gracie in warning because he'd just heard her answer clearly, so he was anxious to see if she would tell the truth.

Taking a deep breath and averting her eyes, she whispered, "The shirt wasn't big enough for me. It was painful, so I…well, I went the wrong way on purpose and hoped you'd tell me to take it off." Peter saw both Jax and Micah stiffen and could hear their jumbled thoughts. They were torn between punishing her for topping from the bottom, lecturing her about the importance of voicing her discomfort, and bailing on dinner altogether to return to their bedroom and fucking her senseless.

Jax leaned over and spoke quietly to his curvy wife, "We'll deal with the underlying issue later—count on that. But for now, I do believe I'd like to change up the order of the toys we'd planned to use." Gracie's eyes went wide as she realized the change probably wasn't going to work out well for her. "I appreciate your honesty, although I have the idea Master Peter didn't leave you with much choice in the matter." The other Doms all chuckled as all three subs cringed. By the time Jax and Micah finished seating the butt plug, every Dom around the table was hard and the scent of their submissive's arousal filled the air. Perhaps they'd been prematurely optimistic to think they could get through a seven-course meal.

LARA KNEW SHE should be looking down like a proper sub, damn it she'd been trained by some of the best Dominants in the country. But holy fucking hell there was no way she could pull her attention away from the scene playing out across the table. Since Masters Fischer and Peter hadn't instructed her to kneel yet, she had a clear view of Gracie bent over the table, her swollen breasts pressing against the mahogany surface, her legs spread apart and her short skirt lifted to bare her curvy ass to the world. Gracie's panted breaths and soft moans floated around the room as her Masters prepared her by rubbing lube into the tight muscles around her rear hole.

Tobi's entire body was flushed with arousal and Lara was grateful to know she wasn't the only one getting turned on just by watching. *Shit, we still have five more courses to serve and the insides of my thighs are already slick.* Yeah, there wasn't going to be anything embarrassing about having evidence of how horny she was trailing down her inner thighs in rivulets—nope nothing embarrassing there. Lara had no idea how Gracie had managed to hold off her orgasm when she'd sounded so close, but her Masters were obviously very proud of her. *Hope that gets her out of the punishment she probably had coming for topping from the bottom.*

Even now, after her own Masters had her kneel between them, Lara saw Micah run his fingers down the side of Gracie's flushed face as she settled between her men. "You know, baby, we weren't going to use that until last. We knew it would make it more challenging for you to walk and didn't want to put you at a disadvantage. But, it's important that you tell us when something is physically uncomfortable for you, it's very difficult for us to care for you without knowing how you are feeling." Even though he hadn't asked her a question, Lara saw Gracie nod her understanding. "We're trained Doms and we do read body language better than most people, but there are only two Doms here who can actually hear what's going on in a sub's mind—and they can't hear the one who belongs to them. If safe, sane, and consensual make up the foundation of our lifestyle, then communication is the bedrock that foundation is built on."

Suddenly Lara knew she and Tobi had been allowed to watch the scene and Gracie's aftercare because their own Doms had wanted them to benefit from the lesson as well. One of the things she loved about the lifestyle was how responsible the Doms felt for the submissive in their care. Hell, they might be demanding at times and over-the-top in their protectiveness of the women they considered *theirs*, but Lara had never met any group of men or women who *nurtured* like the Doms at Dark Desires and Prairie Winds. *Now if I could just convince Peter and Fischer to keep me.*

Chapter Ten

Fischer was finally starting to *hear* a word now and then as thoughts raced through Lara's mind. Perhaps his grandmother had been right when she'd predicted he and Peter's gifts would become more enhanced as their connection to Lara grew. Fischer hadn't been convinced because, quite frankly, he'd been so totally blindsided by his inability to *hear* her. Sure, their granny had always teased them—saying they wouldn't be able to hear "the one" but he'd never really given her taunting much credence. Over the years there had been very few people he hadn't been able to read. As the most gifted of the three Weston brothers, he'd quickly learned anyone he struggled to read was deliberately blocking. And in his experience, the only people who could do that for any extended period of time were sociopaths, and he didn't even want to hear what was going on in their minds.

Lara had been totally turned on watching Jax and Micah with Gracie, but something about the last thought that had run through her mind was what concerned him. He hadn't gotten anything except a sudden rush of insecurity and feeling of loneliness that seemed to have come right out of left field. He pushed it aside for now, because the women were coming from the kitchen, their small serving trays held lettuce wedge salads. Each of them was going in the right direction and he wanted to grin at the determined look on Gracie's face as she rushed around the table despite the large plug her Masters left in her ass, but it was Tobi's thoughts that caught his attention.

Despite the fact Kyle and Kent had described Tobi as hyper-competitive, she also had a heart of pure gold. He knew the precise moment she realized she was going to win this round, then heard her lightning fast decision a split second before she tripped, nearly sending the plates sliding off her tray. The smiles on Kent's and Kyle's faces told Fischer both men knew exactly what their softhearted woman had done and he was sure they would make sure her thoughtfulness was well rewarded.

Tobi knew Lara would have been uncomfortable being the first one completely naked and it would have been particularly uncomfortable when Tobi hadn't lost any pieces of her clothing yet. Despite the fact Fischer didn't know Tobi as well as the other Doms at the table, his affection for her just grew exponentially.

'I can't tell you how many times I've seen her do things like that. Tobi West may be a handful at times, but she is one of the kindest people I've ever met. And right now every Dom at the table wants to pull her into their arms and hug her.' Fischer didn't doubt Peter's words and smiled as Kent and Kyle gently peeled Tobi's shirt from her. When Kent picked up the small, wireless bullet vibe from their basket and popped it into her mouth to warm it, Fischer knew he'd been right—Tobi was about to be rewarded for her sweet gesture.

The salad course took longer than expected because they were all riveted in their seats watching as Kyle and Kent teased Tobi before sending her over the edge. Now that she was leaning against Kyle's leg trembling in the aftermath of a screaming orgasm, the rest of them returned their attention to their meal. When they finished, they all watched as Lara and Gracie walked behind Tobi on their way to the kitchen, they each put a hand on one of her shoulders stilling her attempt to stand. Lara served Kent his sorbet and Gracie served Kyle's, then they each hurried to serve their own Masters. Their solidarity for their friend warmed his heart and he was grateful the two women had taken Lara into their small circle.

The second part of the fourth course's service looked like the Chinese fire drills he and his brothers tortured their parents with at stop signs when they'd been kids, and damned if Fischer didn't want to laugh out loud at their antics. Lara lost, but only by a fraction of a second and he couldn't wait to watch her strip off her skirt.

PETER HELPED LARA settle between them on the cushion, admiring the way her bare breasts lifted with each breath she took. The clamps they'd chosen for her were fairly mild but he'd still heard her hiss of pain at the final turn of the small screw securing the two rings together. While he'd been prepping her and securing the clamps, Fischer had been sliding his fingers through the slick folds of her pussy lips. She didn't know it, but his devious brother had coated his fingers with a stimulating gel, she was likely just now beginning to feel the tingling effects. The sensation would gradually increase in intensity over the next half hour. He was glad her eyes were fixed on the floor when she began fidgeting because hiding his smile was proving to be impossible.

'You really are an evil bastard, you know that?'

'What? I just wanted to add a new dimension to our sweet

sub's training. She's had a pretty easy go of it so far this evening and it was time to shake her up a bit.' Peter knew his brother had known Lara longer, but he wasn't entirely convinced he knew her better—particularly when he glanced down and saw that she was swaying precariously and gasping for breath.

"Lara?" Peter hadn't realized he had practically shouted her name until every other Dom in the room stood, their chairs scraping against the wood floor. He pulled her up by her shoulders and she was practically limp in his hold. *What the hell?* "What's wrong? Tell me. *Now!*" Her entire chest was covered in dark red blotches. He was shocked to see her lips were swollen and she was now gasping for breath.

Turning to Kent, he barked, "Call Kirk or Brian." And then to Kyle, "Call 911." Tobi and Gracie both sprinted from the room, Peter knew they were getting dressed before strangers entered the suite and he wasn't surprised to see Tobi rush back in with a shirt and shorts for Lara before running back down the hall.

He and Fischer had just gotten her into her clothing when Kyle let them know EMS was headed up and Kent shouted, "Kirk's saying he suspects anaphylaxis, probably a reaction to the shrimp. EMS should have epinephrine with them and that should keep her from lapsing into anaphylactic shock." *Why on earth had she eaten something she knew she was allergic to?* The thought had no sooner moved through his mind than he realized she might not have known about her allergy since there likely hadn't been a lot of shrimp served in the dusty villages she'd been raised in.

The next few minutes were as close to chaos as Peter had ever seen outside of his military service, and it certainly wasn't an experience he wanted to repeat. Once the paramedics administered the drug Lara's symptoms began to subside almost immediately. But everyone agreed she should be transported to the hospital to be checked by a physician—well, everyone except their lovely patient, but she was quickly overruled. Even Tobi had leaned over her and shaken her finger saying, "Save it, sister, you're going and that's the end of it."

Five hours later, Peter and Fischer were both ready to pull their hair out. The hospital's emergency department had been indifferent at the least and their lack of interest had bordered on neglect. Kyle had forced Tobi to leave the nurses' station twice when she'd been up in the nurse's face demanding someone attend to Lara. By the end of the second hour, he and Kent had simply stood back and watched with amused expressions while Tobi declared she was calling in reinforcements and dialed Lilly West's number.

Lara was fed up with sitting in the small curtained off room where she was supposed to be "under observation" despite the fact none of them had seen any of the hospital staff in almost two hours. The Charge Nurse was much more interested in managing the growing number of visitors in the waiting room than she seemed to be in her patient. And Peter suspected all hell was about to break loose because he and Jax had both called their fathers who were both members of the hospital's Board of Trustees, and God only knew who Lilly West had called.

LARA PACED THE length of the gurney where she was supposed to be resting and set what she was sure was a record for creative cursing. After the first swat she'd gotten from Fischer, she'd switched to a mixture of tribal dialects—*ha, let him figure that shit out!* Fischer had just shaken his head and laughed, but he hadn't complained about her language after that. "Cupcake, you are going to wear yourself out. Please, at least sit down before Nurse Ratchet comes back in? She will probably be getting at least one phone call about how things are going and I doubt she will be particularly happy about it." Lara had barely had time to register what he'd said when the woman stormed into the area slapping a clipboard on top of the gurney so hard the entire thing slid sideways despite the fact the wheels were locked.

Peter and Fischer moved so quickly they were literally a blur around the gurney before blocking her from the nurse's view. "What on earth is the matter with you two? I'm not going to hurt her. You both need to move out of here and let us do our job." The disdain in her voice made Lara want to slap her silly, but trying to push her way between Peter and Fischer was an exercise in futility.

"You haven't made the slightest attempt to do your job since we arrived so I can't fathom why we should expect anything different from you now. And you'd be well advised to stem the aggressive movements toward our woman, because I'm warning you now—it won't work out well for you." Peter nearly growled at the woman before picking up the clipboard and looking over the paperwork she'd brought along. Lara had to bite her lip to keep from smiling at the woman's shocked expression. *Yeah, that's right. They are both with me. Put that in your pipe and smoke it, bitch.* Lara felt as if her brain had just stuttered—holy hell, she was turning into Tobi. And Fischer's snort of laughter let her know he was indeed beginning to hear her. *Craptastic.*

When the nurse stuck her nose in the air and stormed

out of the small enclosure muttering something along the lines of 'well, I never' Lara was barely able to hold back her laughter. Between Lara's realization that her friends were having a definite influence on her and the older woman's shocked expression, she was biting the inside of her lip to keep from bursting out in giggles. But she lost the battle when Fischer grinned and leaned close to whisper, "I have no doubt she has never—who would want to get that close to her? And it's not about her appearance because quite frankly that doesn't mean jack—but her wounded water buffalo attitude is hideous."

By the time the paperwork was completed and they'd made their way out of the hospital, Lara was too tired to even think about returning to the Wests' hotel suite. "Do you think we could just go on back to the penthouse? I'm sorry I ruined the evening, but I had no idea eating the shrimp would be so dangerous. The last time I had some my cheeks turned bright red, but that was the only reaction I had." The doctor had explained how reactions to food allergies often get exponentially worse with repeated exposure and cautioned her against eating any kind of shellfish in the future.

Peter reached over, taking her hand in his own, "We know you are tired and we're taking you back home. We'll order in something to eat and then get you settled in bed, *mi amõre*."

Fischer leaned over close and whispered, "There likely isn't any dinner left at the suite anyway, since several of the Wests' team went back there a couple of hours ago."

Peter laughed, "And isn't that the truth. Those guys would have made short work of the abandoned food, considering it fair game." They all three laughed because they knew Tobi had sent them back and told them to "take care of things" and no one had any doubt about how the men interpreted that.

Fischer made the call to order their replacement dinner and Peter called to check how things were going at Dark Desires while Lara closed her eyes hoping to rest during the short drive. It seemed like she'd just let her eyes slide closed when she felt herself being lifted into Fischer's arms. She didn't protest, but snuggled closer and enjoyed the feeling of floating until she felt his arms stiffen beneath her. "Take her back downstairs until we know what it is and who brought it." She heard Peter's words but didn't have time to see what he was talking about before the doors closed on the elevator whisking them back down to the lobby.

Fischer must have sensed that she'd awakened, because he pressed a soft kiss to her forehead and whispered, "There was a large envelope leaning against the door, baby. We're just going to be cautious and wait downstairs." It wasn't long before Peter called giving them the all clear. When she started to stand from where they'd been waiting in the lobby, Fischer shook his head and picked her up again. "Before you argue with me, think about the consequences, cupcake. I don't want your bare feet on the floor—it's too cool and this is also a public lobby." Lara didn't argue, but she did find the whole thing amusing—if he'd seen some of the villages where she'd lived, known the unsanitary conditions she'd endured, his opinion of the polished marble floor would probably change substantially.

By the time he set her back on her feet they were well inside the penthouse they shared, Micah and Kent were standing beside Peter frowning at whatever was spread out over the low table in the living room. When she approached, she noticed all three men were wearing latex gloves—definitely not a good sign. As she approached Micah cautioned her to put on a pair of gloves before touching anything, but his words proved to be unnecessary. Once she got close enough to see what they were looking at she froze—her mind reeling in utter disbelief. "How?" was the only thing she managed to utter before Peter pulled her against his side. She didn't know how the other men had gotten here so fast but she was grateful because she felt like her life was spinning out of control so quickly, any and all help was appreciated.

Once she'd finally gotten her bearings, she turned to Peter and asked, "Was there a note?" He nodded and pointed to the neatly printed card balanced on the corner of the table. *We're watching. We want what belongs to us.* The words might not have been an obvious threat, but accompanied by the photos, the meaning was clear—they could have gotten to her at any time. Someone had been watching her for a very long time. After skimming through the first few prints, Lara didn't want to look at any more of the photos and quickly excused herself saying she wanted to take a quick shower and change clothes. And while it was true that she'd always hated the smell of hospitals and was anxious to ride herself of the stench of sickness, blood, and antiseptic that seemed to cling to her hair and clothing, the real issue was she now knew how vulnerable she was. Every suspicion she'd ever had about her parents reared its ugly head and the more she thought about it, the more angry she became. Suddenly she was very anxious to sit down with her grandparents and ask some long overdue questions. She only hoped she wasn't leading trouble to their door.

Chapter Eleven

Peter watched Lara walk down the hall and disappear into their bedroom before turning back to the other three men standing around the table. "How did we miss someone taking pictures of her? Seriously? We're fucking trained operatives? We don't miss this sort of thing. Hell, our lives depend on not missing this shit." He knew his voice was raising, but he couldn't hold back his frustration.

Kent's phone rang before he could continue his tirade and his friend's clipped tone had Peter pausing to listen. "Fuck. When? Well, fine send him up, but make sure he knows we're not stepping back and letting him just take over." Kent ran his fingers through his hair in a gesture of pure frustration after disconnecting the call. He turned to the other men, "Eric Roberts is downstairs having a shit fit and insisting on coming up."

"Christ, that's all we need, a fucking Homeland Security agent crawling up our asses on this when we don't even know what the hell is going on yet." Micah rolled his eyes and started gathering up the pictures. "What's his interest in this anyway? I just can't see this being a national security issue unless we've misinterpreted the puzzle and we aren't looking for diamonds after all."

Fischer turned and headed for the kitchen, "I'm going to set things up so we can feed Lara as soon as the food arrives, she needs to eat something before she crashes." Peter knew Fischer was right, she'd been dead on her feet earlier but he hated the thought of her going to bed without he and Fischer both having a chance to make love to her. Their sweet sub thrived on affection and they intended to make sure she had plenty of it. But now it looked as if all of their plans for this evening were quickly swirling around a drain, ready to be sucked right out from under them both.

Peter opened the front door just as Special Agent Eric Roberts stepped off the elevator alone. The fact he hadn't brought along whoever had drawn the short straw to be his "lackey of the week" was a red flag warning the man might not be acting entirely under the jurisdiction of DHS. Nodding to the man their team had a love-hate relationship with, he held open the door and then followed Roberts inside. "To what do we owe this unexpected pleasure?" Peter knew his tone let the man know exactly how he felt about the interruption, and truthfully, he just simply didn't care.

Kent stood with his back to the large window overlooking the lights of downtown Houston, he made no attempt to soften his question, "What are you doing here, Eric? We told you we'd update you if and when we had something to report."

The agent looked between Peter and Kent, then sighed, "Where are the others?" When Kent simply raised a brow, he shook his head, "Where is Drake? And your brother?" The last was said to Peter, and no one bothered asking how he knew who was in the penthouse because quite frankly it would be a waste of time. The damned man had been an agent a long time despite his youthful appearance and even if he did answer the question it would have been evasive at the very least.

Micah sauntered back in and looked at Eric Roberts like he was pond scum. It was only then that Peter remembered the men shared a mutual dislike for one another, despite the fact they grudgingly admitted that they respected the hell out of each other's computer skills. "Nice to see you too, Micah." Turning back to Peter, he asked, "Your brother?"

"He's busy and you know he isn't involved in agency business, so there isn't any reason to wait for him. Why are you here?" Peter was getting tired of Roberts' questions and he was more than anxious to see him gone before they had to explain to Lara who the hell he was. Not to mention it was going to be damned difficult to explain what the man was doing standing in the middle of their living room this late at night when Peter didn't know himself.

Eric Roberts crossed his arms over his chest, "I'm here because I received a text message earlier this evening warning me to step away from this investigation."

"That can't be that unusual, why pay special attention this time?" Kent's question echoed Peter's own.

"This one also had pictures and it seemed damned odd that you'd allow your lady to have her picture taken in the middle of a medical crisis." Peter felt the earth shift beneath his feet. How could that possibly have happened? How had they been so distracted they hadn't seen someone taking her picture? "Listen, I don't want to stay, I just wanted you to know I'll help if you need it. The chatter is starting to pick up on this thing, somebody wants whatever Lawrence and Rita Emmons have been bringing back to the States and they think Lara has it."

Peter was just opening his mouth to ask if Roberts had any idea what they were looking for when Lara's confused voice sounded behind him, "Simon? What are you doing here?" Peter was so stunned he wasn't even able to speak before her tone become much frostier when she turned to him and asked, "Why didn't you tell me you knew Simon? Oh, drown me. You already knew everything when I finally trusted you enough to share that humiliation, didn't you? Damn, I just never seem to learn."

Looking around, Peter could see that Kent and Micah were staring at Lara, completely baffled by what she'd just said. Fischer stepped into the room and the look on his face was almost as confused. The only person who seemed to know what their sweet woman was talking about was Special Agent Eric Roberts and he had just visibly cringed at Lara's admission that he'd humiliated her. *Wait—did she just call him Simon? What the hell?*

Fischer was glaring at him from across the room and his annoyed words filled Peter's mind, *'Yeah, I was wondering when that little detail was going to register. Man, she is pissed. Figures that the only time I've ever been able to really hear her it's because she is blazing fucking mad.'*

FISCHER STEPPED CLOSER to Lara, but when he noticed the look she gave him, he froze in his tracks. The light that had always been in her eyes when she'd looked at him was gone, it was if he was looking into the eyes of a stranger, someone who had far more reason to distrust him than not. Her expression was all about anger, but the emotion pulsing around her was far worse—she felt as though she'd been betrayed by the men who'd promised to protect and cherish her. He could almost hear her heart ripping apart and it was killing him to stand so far from her.

She turned back to Roberts, "I asked you why you're here. Does this have anything to do with my parents?"

Fischer watched Eric Roberts shift from foot to foot, clearly uncomfortable to have been caught standing in the apartment she shared with he and Peter. At least the ass hat had the decency to realize what a fucking hornet's nest he'd stirred up. "Yes, it does. I'm the agent in charge of the investigation, Lara." When she gasped, he quietly added, "I'm sorry." And with those two words understanding washed over Lara's face and as the truth often does—it finally broke her resolve and tears streamed down her pale cheeks.

"It was always about my parents, wasn't it? Our meeting wasn't coincidental. It was deliberate, and it was always about them, wasn't it? God in heaven I was such a fool. I actually believed you liked me. Damn and double damn, no wonder you asked me a zillion questions about my childhood and all the places I'd traveled to on vacations." She took a deep breath and then another, obviously trying to rein in her emotions before a look of defeat seemed to settle over her, and oddly enough, Fischer instinctively knew that emotion was going to be far harder to fight than her anger. "What is your real name?" When the agent didn't answer quickly enough, she practically snarled the question again, "What is your real name? Damn it you owe me that much."

"Eric Roberts is the name I use in the agency, for all intents and purposes it's real."

"Nice fucking cover, but you know what? I just don't care anymore. You can investigate me, my parents, hell, you can investigate God himself—but you'll do it without my help." And then she simply turned on her heel and walked away. The sound of the bedroom door closing quietly and the soft click of the lock might as well be loud enough to register on the Richter scale for the impact it had. The entire room erupted into angry accusations as he and Peter tried to bring Micah and Kent up to speed.

While they'd been explaining the story to their friends, Fischer watched at Roberts hung his head after Lara had walked away. When he finally looked up, regret was the only thing Fischer could see in the other man's eyes and for just a minute he wondered if perhaps Lara had meant more to him than he'd intended her to. *Well, Mr. Super-Agent, you've not only screwed yourself out of the most amazing woman I've ever known—but I'm not sure you haven't managed to take my brother and me down with you.*

Fischer started to follow Lara, but Peter stopped him, "Give her a little bit of time, brother. She'll come around. We'll just explain that we didn't know Simon Ericson and Eric Roberts were the same person." Peter might be older and he might have traveled the world during his years in the military, but there were times when Fischer wondered how he could be so damned naïve.

'I don't agree, but I want to hear what this prick has to say for himself so I'll wait a few minutes. But I don't think we should leave her alone too long. She's convinced every one of us has sold her out and I don't want her believing that bullshit any longer than she has to.'

It took the better part of an hour to get the story sorted out and by the time they were finished, Fischer was torn between wanting to strangle Simon Ericson for what he'd done to Lara's self-esteem and sympathy for Eric Roberts because it was obvious the man had developed feelings for the young woman who had started out as an assignment. Even sitting across the room from the agent, he was easy to read. *'He knew he'd never have a chance with her after he'd deceived her for so long. If we weren't talking about the woman I want to spend the rest of my life with, I might actually feel sorry for the bastard.'*

Peter had simply nodded in agreement before turning his attention to Kent who had answered his phone and immediately stiffened. "Where is she now?" All conversation had ceased and every eye in the room was on Kent West who was obviously annoyed. "Goddamn woman, what the hell is she thinking?" Fischer was only getting brief pieces from Kent, but he'd gotten enough to know Lara had somehow managed to make it out of the penthouse without being seen. He pulled out his phone and called the one man who would know how their pissed off woman had managed to give them all the slip.

After speaking with Cam, Fischer listened as Kent recounted his conversation with Taz. "Seems your lovely sub found a way out of the penthouse without being seen. Taz was coming back from the coffee shop down the street when he saw her slip out the service entrance. He wouldn't have seen her in the dark alley, but all that lovely blond hair gave her away." Fischer knew Kent was enjoying the fact Lara had thought to dress in dark clothing, but had overlooked the lovely beacon she wore atop her head. "Sorry, but I've seen Tobi make that same mistake more times than I can tell you. She is convinced Kyle and I have night vision, but she never thinks about the fact her hair picks up the dimmest light and magnifies it with every strand. God help us if either of them ever figures it out, and I'd suggest you not mention how he made her."

Fischer knew his friend was trying to lighten the mood because he'd no doubt seen the look on Peter's face. Damn, Fischer wasn't sure he'd ever seen his brother as angry as he was right now. But, what Kent didn't realize was that Peter was angry with himself and with Agent Roberts—the person Kent was trying to shelter from the storm was the only one Peter wasn't angry with.

MICAH HAD BEEN leaning against the mantle over the fireplace watching everything play out around him, but he'd kept the majority of his focus on Eric Roberts. He might not be an empath like the Weston brothers, but it didn't require any special skills to see the man had a serious hard-on for Lara Emmons. He listened as Kent talked to Taz—he didn't need to bother—Micah knew exactly where she was headed, because he'd done his homework. Lara Emmons only had one friend that wasn't associated with the club and he'd read enough of her profile to know she was a submissive to the bone. Every natural sub had a soul that found comfort and pleasure in helping others, so when she was hurting it only made sense that she'd cope by helping someone else.

"Tell Taz if he loses her, to go to the 'Just Like Home Nursing Home' east off The Beltway in Deer Park. She'll be visiting Pearl Betts in room two zero six." Kent simply shook his head and smiled as he relayed the information to Taz. Fischer and Peter were staring at him with a mixture of gratitude and fury, but he'd bet the anger was because they hadn't spent enough time getting to know their woman to know about her elderly friend. But it was Eric Roberts' reaction that was troubling.

Roberts hadn't been surprised and Micah knew the other man well enough to know he'd have left no stone unturned when he'd investigated Lara. But his gut was telling him there was more to it—the man had fallen for the woman he was supposed to view as a suspect and even though Micah didn't believe she was involved in whatever her parents were in to, Roberts didn't have the luxury of giving her the benefit of the doubt. If he was compromised then his decisions all came into question and he'd likely run the risk of being replaced. It was the last issue that bothered Micah the most, simply because it was better to deal with the devil you knew than one you didn't have any experience handling.

Chapter Twelve

Lara knew almost as soon as she stepped out of the building she'd been seen. The years she'd spent in survival mode had finely tuned her sense of self-preservation, so when the fine hairs along the back of her neck stood up, she knew to pay attention. *Damn, she'd been so careful and then to be busted by a giant with coffee.* Hell, she could smell the cups of coffee he was carrying and if she wasn't convinced he'd follow her anyway she'd take the small tray and tell him to get lost.

The drive to the nursing home hadn't given her any opportunities to lose the man following her, although she hadn't tried too hard because she'd decided all things considered, having a bodyguard probably wasn't all bad. He'd sat across the street and watched when she'd stopped at a nearby convenience store to pick up a few of Miss Pearl's favorite treats and then he'd parked a few cars away in the nursing home's large lot. She'd felt him watching as she'd made her way inside, but as soon as she walked in to her elderly friend's room Lara pushed aside everything else and focused on the sweet woman sitting quietly watching her tiny television.

"Hi, Miss Pearl, how are you doing?" Lara plastered on a smile that she hoped would fool the woman who had lived in the same apartment building where Lara had lived before she'd moved into the Barnes' luxurious penthouse.

Miss Pearl's daughter had moved her to the nursing home not long after and then promptly forgotten about her. Miss Pearl's daughter was a selfish twit who pushed her mother to the back burner until she needed money, and then she didn't care if her mom skipped meals for a month or two because she'd generously handed over her social security check. Lara had made fast friends with the sweet older woman who lived across the hall and even though she didn't get to see her daily anymore, she still came by as often as she could. Pulling over the small stool the staff kept for her visits, Lara sat down and handed Miss Pearl the small bag of her favorite candies.

"Lara? It's so late, what are you doing out and about in the city at this hour, my dear?" Lately each visit with Miss Pearl had seemed more important because the older woman was becoming alarmingly frail. The facility provided the best care they could with the money they had, but there wasn't anything of interest for the residents to do with their time. Lara often wondered how many of them simply withered away and died of boredom. She spent the next hour telling the older woman about her scare with the shrimp—leaving out many of the details of the dinner. Miss Pearl knew Lara worked at Dark Desires, but they'd never discussed any of the details of her personal participation. Her older friend might be incredibly open-minded, but Lara didn't think she was quite ready to hear all the intimate details of her ménage lifestyle.

"Were you having dinner with those two hotties of yours? Good Lord, but I'd like to get a look at them—it's just not the same seeing men on this little television." Lara laughed out loud, maybe she needed to bring Miss Pearl to one of the club's Meet and Greet events, there were actually a couple of widowed men her age who attended each month's get-together. "But I don't think your visit to the emergency room is what's sent you to see an old woman in the middle of the night, is it?" When the older woman's wrinkled hand grasp her own much smoother one—and it was that casual gesture of love and support that was Lara's undoing.

Grabbing a small bottle of lotion, Lara gently massaged Miss Pearl's dry hands and let her tears fall as she told her friend about seeing Simon again and the betrayal she'd felt when she'd discovered he'd never really been interested in her and that everyone around her seemed to already know the man. As the story poured out and Lara answered Miss Pearl's occasional question, she had to admit the men had all seemed surprised she'd known Simon, but they certainly didn't act as though he was a stranger and she'd needed to put space between herself and the whole mess so she could think clearly. God she was grateful CeCe had told her about the Panic Room and the hidden exit in the master suite. Lara was surprised they'd left her in the room alone long enough for her to utilize the safety feature Cameron Barnes had installed in his home.

When she finally wound down and looked up at Miss Pearl, her friend was watching her with kind eyes surrounded by deep laugh lines speaking of a lifetime spent making others smile. Miss Pearl's dark eyes never seemed to miss even the smallest detail and Lara had never known her to be wrong in her assessments of people or situations. "Well, I saw you with Simon and I can assure you the man was quite smitten." She held up her hand when Lara started to protest, halting the argument, "I understand that his intentions weren't honorable and that he obviously wouldn't know the truth if he walked into it face first, but I know what I saw. He fell for you but you can bet your bottom dollar he knew he didn't stand a chance with that web of lies he'd spun closing in on him."

Miss Pearl just waited, giving Lara a chance to think about what she'd said before asking, "Tell me, would you have given him the time of day after finding out what he'd done? Even if he'd told you he'd fallen in love with you in the process?" When Lara shook her head, Miss Pearl smiled, "Of course not, and he had to have known that as well. And you know how fragile men's egos can be—he'd have walked away before facing that loss. Now, about your two hotties—honey-girl, you owe it to them to at least listen to what they have to say. Don't you suppose they are worried about you being out alone this late?" Lara noticed Miss Pearl looked over her shoulder but didn't turn around because it wasn't unusual for the staff to stick their heads in to confirm who was visiting.

"No. One of their team saw me leaving and followed me, so I'm sure they know I'm safe. And since someone out there is under the mistaken impression my parents sent me something valuable, I'm willing to concede that I need help. But I'm not sure how much I trust anyone right now. How do I know whether or not they are with me because they want to be or simply because they are a part of the investigation?" She felt another tear roll slowly down her cheek and found herself leaning into Miss Pearl's touch when the older woman cupped her cheek with her cool palm.

"Honey, trust your heart. You may experience pain now and then, but the joy will outshine the darkness. Remember, you can't truly appreciate the mountains unless you've seen the valleys. Take a chance that there are mountains beyond this valley, sweetheart—I promise you won't regret it." Miss Pearl leaned forward and pressed a soft kiss against Lara's forehead and then quietly added, "Now, honey, it's past my bedtime and I do believe there are a couple of young men here to collect you." Lara spun around on the small stool and gasped at the sight of Peter and Fischer both leaning against the doorframe. They filled the door and once again Lara found herself almost mesmerized by their appearance.

Lara had lost track of the number of times she'd found herself staring at them struck speechless, but it was more than their physical attractiveness—which was remarkable itself. But both men had a *presence* that drew people to them. Perhaps it was their unique ability to hear the thoughts of others—did that give them such an advantage understanding others that people sensed the connection? Peter stepped forward to kneel in front of Miss Pearl, introducing himself and then his brother. Fischer held out his hand to her and Lara didn't hesitate to place her much smaller hand in his larger one, and the first touch reminded her why she'd trusted them from the beginning. Even though the first touch always sent a zing of electricity up her arm, it was the sense of security that always lingered that she found the most attractive.

FISCHER DIDN'T EVEN realize he was holding his breath until Lara placed her hand in his without even a heartbeat of hesitation. Relief swept through him knowing that her trust in them hadn't been completely destroyed simply because of their association with Eric Roberts. He wasn't a fool, Fischer knew full well that it wouldn't matter that he'd never actually met the man, the fact Peter knew him could have easily been enough to sink them both. "Come on, baby, you look completely spent. Peter will say your goodbyes and be out in a few minutes."

What he wasn't going to say—yet, was that Peter was talking to Lara's friend about moving to another facility. When Micah had told them what he'd learned about the elderly woman's situation, they'd made a couple of calls and could have Mrs. Pearl Betts moved in to a beautiful new assisted living apartment by noon tomorrow if she was willing to go. After learning how Ms. Betts had befriended the lonely college coed living across the hall from her, caring for her when she'd been ill, encouraging her to continue her education, and helping her learn to safely navigate their neighborhood, there wasn't anything Peter and Fischer weren't willing to do to make the last years of her life more pleasant.

Just as they walked out the front door of the nursing home, Lara sighed deeply, "I hate it that she has to live here. There isn't a single activity for her, she sits in her room day and night watching that ridiculously small television—she is bored to distraction." Fischer wasn't sure Lara even realized she'd spoken out loud.

Using the hand he was holding to spin her into his arms, he looked down into her eyes and smiled, "Cupcake, Peter is talking to your friend about that very thing right now. We were going to wait and surprise you, but you've already got so much on your plate, I don't want you worrying over this any longer. If she'll let us, we'll have her in one of the nicest retirement villages in the city and I promise you there will be so many things to keep her busy you'll have to make an appointment to visit her." The gratitude and relief he saw in her expression made his heart squeeze, knowing such a small gesture on their part had made such an impact on Lara spoke to the type of person she was at her core.

"I don't know how I'll ever be able to thank you. She wouldn't let me help her, but I have a feeling Peter won't take no for an answer—and I can't tell you how happy I am about that." He pulled her close wrapping his arms around her and just enjoyed the feel of her curves pressing against him. Worrying he'd never hold her again had terrified him and hugging her was as much about his own comfort as it was about hers.

"We're happy to help, what use is money if you don't use it to help others?" Money was an issue they'd be discussing at some point in the very near future because one of the things the investigation had turned up was the fact several incredibly large deposits had been made during the previous two years to Lara's trust fund account. There was no evidence that she knew about the deposits since she seemed inclined to completely ignore the fact she even had a trust fund. All of the details were handled by her family and from what Micah had been able to uncover, Lara was under the mistaken impression that her mother was estranged from her family, when in fact they'd spoken several times during the past several years. Why her parents had hidden that fact was just another question to add to the growing list he was hoping their visit to her grandparents' estate would be able to clear up.

Fischer could read the satisfaction in Peter's expression when he emerged from the nursing home to join them on the sidewalk despite the glare he gave Fischer, "Is there some reason you have our woman standing out in the cool night air?" *'Completely exposed to anyone who might want to take a pot-shot at her?'*

"Yes, as a matter of fact there is—I wanted to hug her." *'Can it. She and I both needed this moment, or have you forgotten that we have some ground to make up thanks to your pal, Eric Roberts?'* Walking Lara the rest of the way to the Towne Car they had waiting, he held out his hand for her keys and tossed them to Taz before helping her into the dark interior of their car.

Once he'd settled in beside her, he leaned over and snapped her seatbelt in place before securing his own and enclosing her soft hand in his own. "We'll be home soon and then you really need to eat something before you sleep, baby. We're going to push back our trip to your grandparents' estate a couple of hours because we're worried about you." He saw her eyes sparkle with questions, but he wasn't willing to argue the point with her. "No, cupcake. This is not open to discussion. We'll sort everything else out tomorrow, including the fact you put yourself in danger by leaving this evening. But we will do it after you've allowed us to take care of you—you'll eat and rest first. We'll go see your grandparents and perhaps find some answers about this mess that seems to be building like a damned tsunami wave."

This time she didn't attempt to argue and before they'd even gotten out of the parking lot she had unfastened her seat belt and curled up in his lap. Fischer felt as if his heart was going to explode with gratitude because he'd been terrified at the devastation he'd seen in her eyes just a couple of hours ago. He wasn't sure what all Pearl Betts had said to Lara, but the woman had definitely cemented her place at the top of their most favored vanilla friends list.

Fischer knew the minute Lara's mind finally shut down and she fell asleep cuddled against him with the top of her head tucked under his chin because her entire body sagged in relief from her utter exhaustion. Once their driver parked in front of the building where they lived, Peter opened the door and Fischer gently laid her in Peter's waiting arms before climbing out of the car. "She's had an unbelievably difficult day, yet she took time to stop and buy Ms. Betts a sack of her favorite candies. I'm not sure I've ever met anyone like her." Fischer appreciated the almost reverent tone in Peter's voice and his own thoughts echoed those of his older brother, except he wasn't convinced there *was* anyone like her.

Chapter Thirteen

Peter loved carrying Lara, she'd opened her eyes briefly as they'd stepped into the elevator, a small smile lifted the corners of her full lips but then her eyelids slid closed as she sighed contentedly. There was no greater feeling for a Dom than being trusted by the submissive in their care and a feeling of utter contentment moved through him. Trying to wake her so she could eat something proved to be a battle they decided wasn't worth fighting. They quickly abandoned the idea, opting instead to use those few moments she was half-awake to get her undressed and settled in the middle of their large bed. By the time they'd both finished showering, she was once again sleeping deeply.

The trip to her grandparents' estate north of Houston seemed to take forever and Peter wondered more than once what was going through Lara's mind as she stared out the windows of the car. *'I hate the hesitation I see in her eyes. She doesn't trust her family anymore and I'm not sure that I blame her.'* He and Fischer had let Kent and Micah take the lead briefing Lara this morning on what they'd learned about her trust fund and he'd seen the disbelief in her eyes. The implications were too obvious to need mentioning aloud, and from that moment on, he'd noted she seemed to be slowly slipping away from them.

Lara's emotional detachment would have to be dealt

with quickly, but right now she was already dealing with a barrage of unsettling information and he knew there was nothing to be gained by adding to her burden. He left her to her own thoughts but continued watching her out of the corner of his eye, not wanting to let her sink too far into self-doubt. Knowing when to step back and when to intercede with a sub had never been an issue before, but not being able to connect with Lara as an empath was presenting more challenges than he'd ever anticipated. *'Are you able to hear her yet?'* He knew Fischer had connected briefly the night before at the penthouse, but he wasn't sure his brother was still able to hear her.

'Not like I want to, but I'm getting stronger impressions of her emotions. Damn I wish Adam wasn't out of the country. We could really use his help.' The oldest Weston brother was married to Cecelia Barnes' sister and Adam had taken Camille and their young children on an extended vacation immediately following her sister's wedding. Adam was an empath as well, and they hoped he'd be able to give them some insight with Lara. Adam hadn't been able to *hear* Camille for a long time, but since he nor Fischer had ever had any trouble, they'd hoped he'd be able to help.

'I agree and the rat-bastard had the nerve to laugh at me when I called him to find out for sure when they planned to return. Hell, I never did get an answer. I swear I think we should worship the ground our saint of a sister-in-law walks on for taking him off the family's hands.' Peter could almost feel Fischer's laughter at his words.

When he turned to Lara, he saw she was watching him, the corners of her lips tilted up ever so slightly. "I can tell when you two are doing that you know. The air around you almost crackles with a really weird static electricity, it gives you away every time." Peter was completely stunned and seeing Fischer turn around to gape at her from the passenger seat in front of them let him know his brother was just as shocked. Lara's eyes became wary as she appeared to push back into the seat, "What?"

"No—it's okay. We're just surprised—very pleasantly surprised I should add. It's really rare to find anyone who can sense what you just described—we've never had that happen with anyone who wasn't gifted." Peter reached over to take her hand in his and couldn't hold back how right everything about her felt as he pressed a kiss against her slender fingers. "It just proves how perfect you are for us."

WHEN THE DRIVER turned through the stately brick and wrought iron gates onto the lane leading to her grandparents' estate, Lara felt memories assail her. Looking out over the track that circled the large front lawns, Lara fondly remembered riding the ponies her grandfather kept for her. Looking out over the track she knew if she closed her eyes she'd practically be able to feel the wind blowing through her hair the one and only time she was allowed to ride one of her grandfather's full sized horses. She'd ridden ponies for years, but it was that one brief sprint around the track on a regular horse before her grandmother had come storming down the front steps of their stately mansion like a Category 5 hurricane that she remembers best—and it had been enough to hook her forever. And even though she hadn't ridden in more years than she wanted to count, she'd never forgotten the joy she'd found in those precious few minutes.

"*Mi amōre*? Are you all right?" Peter's softly whispered

question brought her back to the moment and when she turned away from the window to face him, he reached over and gently wiped away the tears she hadn't even realized were falling. She wasn't sure why she was so emotional, she hadn't seen her grandparents in a very long time. She'd been told there had been some sort of falling out between her parents and grandparents, and rather than getting pulled into the drama, Lara had opted for the good old Ostrich Theory and simply avoided it altogether. In hindsight, that seemed like a terribly selfish and cowardly decision, but there wasn't anything to do about that now, so she tried not to get tangled up in the emotions of guilt and regret.

"I am, or at least I will be. But I appreciate you asking. I just got caught up in a memory." She didn't want to tell them how much she'd longed for some sort of family connection—how much she envied the fact they had each other and an older brother they both seemed to admire. She'd met the Weston family a couple of times and they seemed like lovely people, but she'd felt like an outsider despite how welcoming they had been. The bottom line was without a commitment from Peter and Fischer, she simply didn't feel like she was a part of their family. And thanks to her parents' nonsense with her grandparents, she didn't really feel as if she was a part of her own family either.

Lara's physical appearance had made her an outsider in every village her family had lived in and her lack of knowledge of the social mores of U.S. schools had kept her from ever being accepted once she'd started high school. And for someone with a submissive personality—whose soul craved acceptance, it was like living in the seventh level of hell. The friends she'd made at Dark Desires were the closest thing she had to family now—*and isn't that about as pathetic as it gets. What kind of person centers their life around a kink club? One that needs to get themselves together, that's who.* Well fuckity fuck, now she was not only talking to herself, but she was answering too—*great.*

Until they parked behind another large black car matching the one she was riding in, Lara had forgotten that Jax and Kent had come up early to talk with her grandparents while Micah and Kyle stayed downtown with Gracie and Tobi. John and Elizabeth Hunt had been friends with both Jax and Kent's families for many years and when they offered to lay some of the groundwork for her, Lara had jumped at the opportunity. Jax stepped out of the massive wooden doors to stand on the mansion's large front porch just as the car came to a stop. But Lara barely noticed him, her eyes locked on the elderly couple standing to his side and it felt as if all the air had suddenly been sucked out of the car.

Somewhere in the distance Lara heard Peter's concerned voice asking her if she was all right but she couldn't focus on anything except the faces of the grandparents she'd loved so much as a child. How had she let so many years slip away without coming to see them? The realization of what she'd lost slammed into her and it wasn't until Peter put his hands on either side of her face and physically turned her face to his did she realize she wasn't even breathing. "Damn it, Lara—take a breath. Come on, sweetheart, breathe with me." She felt herself take a gasping breath, but he shook his head, "No, princess. Slow and easy. Come on, three counts in and then three out. Follow me. Focus now, let's get you settled before we join the others."

Peter's hands still bracketed her face when she finally

felt her breathing level out and the pounding of blood quieted in her ears, it was only then that she realized they were alone in the car. When she finally looked back out the window, Lara saw that Fischer was shaking hands with her grandparents and warm smiles had replaced the tense expressions that she'd seen earlier. Nodding when Peter asked her if she was ready, Lara took a deep breath and placed her hand in Peter's as she stepped from the car.

FISCHER INTRODUCED HIMSELF to Lara's grandparents and was overjoyed to discover they seemed to be as honest and open as Jax and Kent had remembered. Even though he didn't ask them any specific questions about their daughter or son-in-law, it was obvious their granddaughter was the center of their focus. He wasn't trying to pick up specific thoughts because the energy around them was so open he didn't feel it was necessary—as long as they didn't appear to be a threat to Lara, he and his brother had agreed to respect their privacy.

"Is she okay? We were positively thrilled when Jax called. To be honest we'd almost given up hope we'd get a chance to see her again. Heaven only knows what sort of nonsense her parents have told her." Fischer wasn't sure if Elizabeth Hunt was speaking to him, her husband, or herself because her gaze hadn't moved from her granddaughter as they all watched Peter calm her.

"She'll be fine, she was just a bit overcome by memories as we came up the driveway." When John stiffened, Fischer added, "I'm not sure she'd expected all the fond memories that came over her, she'd just been a little overwhelmed, she'll be fine. Let's just give Peter a chance to settle her a bit." Both of them nodded quickly, Fischer was grateful he wasn't forced to elaborate because at this point he wasn't sure exactly who he'd been trying to convince.

'What's going on? How long is this going to take? Do you need me to come back to the car?'

'Christ, put a lid on it, Fischer. We'll be there in just a minute. I want her to get some color back in her face, because right now she'd so pale her skin is almost translucent.' Fischer continued to listen as Peter coaxed Lara to synchronize her breathing with his own. As the middle brother, Peter had often been the mediator and Fischer fought his smile as he thought back on how those skills were still evident today. Keeping everyone around him calm was one of the things Peter did best and he was doing a damned fine job of it with Lara. Pointing out her grandparents' worried expressions and assuring her that Fischer, Jax, nor Kent would never let her walk into an unsafe situation, Peter was finally able to get her to exit the car.

Fischer watched Lara walk hand in hand with Peter up the wide marble staircase lost in appreciation for the fact she belonged to them when it suddenly hit him that neither he nor Peter had ever told her exactly how they hoped the future would play out. And that brief moment of insight made him realize how lax they'd become—it was something every Dom knew to avoid and they'd done it with the only woman who'd ever really mattered. They failed to give the most important woman in the world—the one they wanted to keep forever—the security of knowing how committed they were to her long-term. Nothing could have held him back at that moment, descending the last few steps to meet her, Fischer stood directly in front of Lara taking her free hand in his and using his other hand to gently lift her chin so he could hold her gaze.

"Baby, I want you to know that nothing is going to happen today that will change the way Peter and I feel about you. Nothing short of your out-right rejection will keep us from keeping you in our lives forever." When her pretty blue eyes went wide he knew he'd been right. "That's right, cupcake, you belong to us. I'm sorry we hadn't laid that out before—but that's on us, not you." The relief in her expression was so clear Fischer wasn't sure whether to kick his own ass for causing her to worry or to praise whatever angel had just whispered in his ear alerting him to a problem that was so easily resolved. Pressing a quick kiss to her lips, he turned and the three of them ascended the final steps together.

Chapter Fourteen

Four hours later Lara felt as if she'd never been gone. The easy rapport she'd once had with both her grandmother and grandfather had been so easy to reestablish she wondered why her parents had been so eager to deny her the joy of spending time with them, but she also wondered why she'd allowed it. Her parents had managed to convince her the grandparents she'd loved so dearly had suddenly decided they didn't want anything to do with her and she'd bought the story, lock, stock, and barrel. But the burning question remained, why had they wanted her kept from a couple who had so obviously adored her? Lara's best guess was her grandparents had started asking all the same questions she was now asking.

She hadn't even realized she was staring vacantly out the large leaded glass windows of the dining room until her grandfather stepped up beside her and took her hand in his. When she turned to look at him, Lara was surprised to see understanding in his dark eyes. "You're thinking awfully hard over here, princess. Come on, let's you and I go for a walk." Lara followed him out the door enjoying the feeling of his strong hand holding hers. His hand might have been more wrinkled than hers, but she knew each of those wrinkles proved the self-made millionaire was no stranger to hard work. Having started out as a wildcatter in the oil fields, John Hunt had built a virtual empire by the time he'd turned forty. By his fiftieth birthday he's expanded the business in so many directions it was hard to find a pie he hadn't had his fingers in.

Smiling up at him as they stepped out onto the cobblestone walkway that would lead them through her grandmother's beautiful floral gardens, Lara asked, "Why? I mean, do you know what they were thinking?" When he didn't immediately respond, she continued, "I keep wondering why they didn't want me to come here when we moved back to the U.S. I feel cheated and I'm guessing you do too."

"Oh, you have no idea how much. And we wanted to contact you so many times, but your mother...well, let's just say she was adamant that we not. Her threats were credible because unfortunately she'd made a lot of very unsavory contacts over the years." Leading her to a small bench, they sat down and looked out over a beautiful pool with a two-story tall waterfall watching the cool mist drift away as water tumbled over the natural stone structure. The landscaping was breathtaking and Lara couldn't help but feel calmed by the soft sounds of falling water. She remembered reading once that falling water altered the ions in the air causing people to feel more settled and happier—it was easy to believe that as she let the peacefulness of her surroundings move over her in slow comforting waves.

"I'm sure that you've figured out by now that your parents are far more than simple missionaries." When she nodded, he smiled, "I didn't think that knowledge would elude you forever, and I knew the minute Jax called he was more than a little suspicious. When we found out, we pleaded with your parents to let you come back to the States and stay with us. We even flew to Athens to meet them in hopes they'd let us bring you back home where you'd be safe."

Lara was shocked. She remembered the holiday they'd spent in Athens when she'd been twelve or thirteen, but she hadn't had any idea her grandparents were in the same city. "How did you find out?" She knew she wouldn't have to explain the question, her grandfather was obviously an astute businessman so he'd understand exactly what she was asking.

"There had been clues for a long time, and I'd instituted a number of security protocols over the years so any unusual financial activity involving you would immediately send up red-flags. My staff includes some rather gifted computer experts and I assure you they don't miss anything." He chuckled before turning a much more serious expression to her, "Sweetheart, when deposits started being made to a trust fund I'd established for you—deposits I hadn't made—that set off all of our alarms. One of the guys likened it to standing in the middle of a casino when every one-armed bandit in the place hit the jackpot." Suddenly his expression changed and for the first time Lara got a glimpse of the shrewd businessman who'd single-handedly created an empire.

"Well, I moved the money—all of the money, into a different account out of the country." His predatory smile told her that he'd been intentionally trying to flush out information he'd likely already had. "Needless to say, it didn't take long before my son-in-law called demanding to know what I'd done with *his wife's* money. Well, the way I saw it, they'd put that money in an account with someone else's name on it, an account they weren't even supposed to know existed." When she looked surprised, he chuckled. "From the very start I wasn't that impressed with your dad.

I knew who he worked for before he and your mother ever left Washington D.C. but she'd managed to convince us he'd given up working for Uncle Sam—as it turns out, he'd simply recruited her."

Lara knew she should be surprised, but in truth she wasn't. Her mother was absolutely brilliant and had been utterly devoted to her father, she would have followed him to the ends of the earth—hell, she *had*. Rita Hunt had given up a promising modeling career to marry and move to the most remote places in the world. And while their time in each place had always been relatively short, most of the locations had been little more than wide places in the road—and calling many of those trails roads was being charitable. She'd once heard her mother say that their frequent vacations had been the only thing that made it all worthwhile, but then she'd laughed and added "and the money of course" which hadn't made any sense to Lara at the time because she sure didn't see any of the trappings of wealth. Of course now that she thought back on it, most missionaries probably didn't have satellite phones and encrypted laptops either.

"Do you have any idea where they might have hidden whatever it is someone is after? I mean, well…someone thinks I know and I really have no clue. The only clue I have led me here." What she didn't say was that she'd be forever grateful that she'd been forced to reconnect with her grandparents, and she didn't have any intention of letting anything come between them again.

"I don't, not really. To my knowledge, neither your mother nor your father has been to the estate for a long time. But I can tell you the last time they were here, they spent most of their free time in the stables, and that was unusual because neither one particularly liked horses." He looked up at her and grinned, "But you, princess, you were my golden girl with the ponies. God you loved them and they loved you, too. It almost killed me when your grandmother made you stop riding. She was so sure I was going to let you break your neck."

"I remember, and I missed riding. Do you still have horses?" She'd tried to keep the hopeful tone from her voice, but knew she'd failed when his eyes lit up like lights in Shepherd Park Plaza at Christmas. He didn't even answer, he just grabbed her hand and pulled her to her feet hurrying toward the stables. She didn't even try to hold back her laughter, "I'm taking this as a yes."

"Oh, yes indeed. And I had the fellas working in the stable saddle up a couple of mounts in hopes you might remember how much fun it was to ride." Lara felt tears burn the back of her eyes at his thoughtfulness. And even though she hadn't ridden in years, she wasn't about to disappoint him by turning down the chance to enjoy a few minutes sharing his love of horses. She'd missed far too many special moments with them and she wasn't about to miss any more now that she was getting a second chance.

By the time they'd finished their ride an hour later, Lara already felt the muscles in her thighs burning. Her groan as she swung her leg over the back of the mare she'd been riding turned to a startled squeak when large hands wrapped around her waist and set her gently on the ground. Turning, she looked up into Peter Weston's turquoise green eyes, "*Mi amōre*, did you have a good time?" The affection in his eyes and in his voice was unmistakable and she leaned against him, enjoying how right it felt to be in his arms. She loved hearing his heart beating beneath her ear and inhaled deeply, relishing his masculine scent. Lara wasn't sure what had caused her to suddenly seek comfort in his arms, perhaps it was simply the emotional rollercoaster she'd been riding the past few days.

Leaning back, she smiled, "I did. I'd forgotten how much I loved riding, but I already know I'm going to pay for it tomorrow. I'm embarrassed to admit how much my muscles are already protesting."

"Well, while you were out, we looked around the stables and there are a couple of things we'd like to show your grandfather." He saw disappointment in her eyes and he knew exactly where her mind had gone. When she turned to walk into the stables, Peter pulled her back effortlessly. "No, sweetness it probably isn't anything important, and it certainly isn't something your grandfather would have noticed. But one of the stable hands pointed out a couple of boards that didn't seem to match the others and we'd like permission to see if there is a reason for that."

"Why don't you think my grandfather would have noticed?" She certainly didn't want to think he was involved, especially after he'd seemed so sincere earlier when he'd told her how they'd worried about her safety. But the simple fact was, she didn't know the man anymore and she didn't have the best track record when it came to judging people.

"These boards are way in the back of the building and up higher than he'd have been able to see without using a ladder. The only reason the men who work here noticed is because they had to repair one of the lights a few weeks ago and that put them close enough to see the difference in the wood. Evidently that part of the loft is generally concealed by the small bales of feed your grandfather buys to feed the horses, so it's hard to tell exactly when the boards were replaced. It also answers the 'feed at eleven' part of the puzzle because if you stand at the door and look up at the eleven o'clock position, you'd find that spot immediately—behind the feed."

Taking her hand, he began leading her back to the house, "Come on, your grandmother wants to spend some time with you also. She's been fussing that your granddad was keeping you all to himself—just like he used to do when you were younger, according to her." His laughter at her grandmother's complaints made Lara smile because she remembered this being a familiar argument. "She really is a remarkable woman, precious girl. I'm looking forward to getting to know them both."

They'd made it about halfway back to the house when he stopped her and brushed the hair away from her face. "We can read them, you know—and they are exactly what they seem to be, *mi amõre*. They are overjoyed you are back in their lives and they'll move heaven and earth to keep you safe." He laughed then and leaned down so his words warmed the shell of her ear, "Elizabeth Hunt is a force of nature. She gave both Fischer and I the third degree about our intentions—hell, Kent wants to hire her as an interrogator."

FISCHER STAYED ON the ground with John Hunt while Jax and Kent climbed up to investigate the boards that had been pointed out to them. Lara's grandfather hadn't hesitated to give them permission to pull the boards loose, he'd insisted the men working in the stable were the only ones with keys aside from the one that was in the house and the one on his key ring. When he'd admitted he hadn't used the spare that was kept in their kitchen for years, a quick phone call to the house confirmed what Fischer had suspected—the key was missing.

Jax was nailing the boards back in place as Kent moved down the ladder he'd climbed to help. Walking over to John Hunt, Fischer noticed a small red envelope in his hand. "John, any idea what this key might fit?" Fischer knew Kent already had an idea, but he was waiting to hear the older man's opinion.

John took the envelope, let a strange looking key fall into his hand and studied it carefully. "Looks like a safe deposit key to me, but I'm sure it's not mine. We gave up our bank boxes when we built the vault in our basement about ten years ago, and what isn't there is in a separate vault at the law office we've always used for personal business."

When Jax joined them, he asked, "Did the note mean anything to you?" At the older man's raised brow, Jax took the envelope from his hand and turned it over reading the beautifully scripted note, "This key will unlock your heart." Looking up at John, he asked again, "Does that mean anything to you at all? My guess is the key word there is heart."

John seemed to consider Jax's question as they slowly began making their way back up to the Hunts' large mansion. They'd almost reached the patio where the others were waiting when John stopped and said, "I met Elizabeth when she worked at the Heart of Texas Bank downtown. I know Rita always thought that story was romantic, so I'm guessing she's trying to tell us where the box is located that this key will open." Yeah, that was Fischer's guess as well, the million-dollar question was, what was in the box that had set this damned scavenger hunt in motion?

Elizabeth Hunt was a typical Southern lady and insisted they eat dinner before making any decisions. But the truth was, after seeing the buffet she and her cook had put together it hadn't taken much to convince any of them to stay. Jax leaned back in his chair and groaned, "Miss Elizabeth, you have nearly rendered me useless. I'm not sure I'll even be able to walk to the car let alone fold myself inside." When she waved him off, he laughed, "Thank you. It was amazing and I'm going to have great fun rubbing it in to my mom that your apple fritters are better than hers."

"Don't you dare, I swear I'll take a switch to you myself if you do. I'll never get invited to another of her cooking parties—and those are very coveted invitations, you know." Her mock horror had Jax throwing his head back and laughing out loud. From what Fischer understood, the two women had been friends for years and their friendly cooking competitions were some sort of legend among their small inner circle. Fischer held back his laughter when he thought back on Lara's numerous cooking catastrophes—clearly their lovely woman had missed out on the cooking gene.

Chapter Fifteen

Lara had become somewhat desensitized to double takes over the years, her long, wavy light blond hair, petite curves, and gregarious nature meant she often caught the attention of both men and women. But today she was garnering more notice than usual because of the men surrounding her as she walked into the bank. Fischer was often teased about his movie star looks for good reason, and with Peter being not far behind—both literally and in appearance, women were tripping over themselves to look at them. Her grandfather was very distinguished looking as well, and he'd laughed when she'd said he looked dapper in his tailored three-piece suit.

All the attention was so utterly ridiculous she was having trouble holding back her laughter. Her grandfather met them at the curb and escorted her inside while Fischer was at her other side. Peter was following them, having told her he had her "six", which Fischer had explained it meant he'd be watching her backside—Lara figured that it was either some sort of military lingo or guy code for looking at her ass.

Jax McDonald was standing just inside the entrance, which meant Kent and the man they called Taz had probably been outside watching them even though she hadn't seen them. Jax was standing next to a man who kept looking nervously at her grandfather and for the first time

Lara truly noticed how enormous Jax was. Every other time she'd seen him standing close to another man, it had been a member of the Prairie Winds team and they were all so tall his height hadn't seemed so startling. But now, standing next to the man who her grandfather introduced as the bank's president, Jax seemed every inch of his almost seven foot height—it was no wonder the poor man leading them to the safe deposit box area seemed so nervous.

While the bank president spoke quietly with the woman at the counter, Lara glanced over at her grandfather, she could see he was fighting a smile. Lara let her eyes ask the silent question and his grin widened as he leaned closer, "Frederick had the hots for your grandmother, but I stole her right out from under him. I keep money in this bank just so I can rub it in his nose occasionally." For the first time Lara got a glimpse of the *man* beneath her image of him as her grandfather and she realized they could easily become very close if she'd just let her guard down.

Leaning over, she pressed a quick kiss too his wrinkled cheek, "It's easy to see why she chose you." His pale blue eyes became glassy with unshed tears that he quickly blinked away and his whispered "thank you" warmed her heart.

It didn't take long to determine the key did indeed fit a box in their safe, once they'd all crowded into the small private room used for those wanting to access their valuables, Lara flipped open the lid and gasped. It wasn't just the contents of the box that shocked her, but she was immediately struck by the magnitude of the problem she was facing. People had been killed for a lot less than lay in a rectangular metal container on the counter in front of her. *Missionaries my sweet ass…*

PETER PRIDED HIMSELF on rarely being surprised by the crazy shit people did—up until this moment he had honestly believed years of being privy to their thoughts meant there wasn't anything he hadn't seen or *heard*. But he'd been wrong—very, very wrong. There were several small clear plastic bags filled with various sizes of what appeared to be cut diamonds and more bags of uncut gems as well. Beneath those were bearer bonds—lots of them. While the gems were valuable, they were likely going to be eclipsed by the bonds that were the financial instruments of choice for anyone trying to conceal their business transactions and evade the IRS. Hell, Peter had been on more than one op involving money laundering and he knew how often these bonds were used to move huge sums of money from point A to criminal B.

"Pretty easy to see why the agency has been so interested in Lara's parents." Peter wanted to laugh at Jax's understatement, but the simple fact was her parents had painted an enormous target on their only child. Hell, just having the key was dangerous, Jax's voice brought him back to the moment, "Christ, what were they thinking setting her up like this? Damn we didn't bring enough backup to get this out of here, I'm not even comfortable leaving with the key." And as if the Universe had heard him, Jax's phone rang. His frown got Peter's attention but he didn't have time to tell Lara what he was hearing before Jax ended the call. "Let's get this back in the safe right now, people. We've got company coming."

Just as they walked out of the bank's vault area they came face to face with Special Agent Eric Roberts. Peter felt Lara stiffen beside him, "What are you doing here?"

"Good morning, Lara. Is this your grandfather? Special Agent Eric Roberts, sir." Roberts extended his hand but sensing his granddaughter's hostility John Hunt simply raised his eyebrow and looked at Roberts as if he was some sort of insect. Yeah, Peter was liking John Hunt more by the minute.

'Damn, I really like our woman's gramps. Easy to see where she gets her moxy.' Peter agreed with Fischer's assessment and he looked forward to getting to know the older man.

'I couldn't agree more. What the fuck does Roberts want and how did he know we were here?'

'I don't know, but I'll bet your team is scrambling to find out.' And wasn't that an understatement? Peter was betting the Prairie Winds team was mobilizing quickly, they'd be pulling together in a big hurry, but in the meantime, Peter felt sure the West brothers were calling in local favors and they'd have backup rolling in hot and fast very soon.

Lara turned to her grandfather and briefly explained how she'd met Special Agent Roberts. The more she explained the angrier her grandfather looked until Peter was actually starting to feel sorry for Roberts as he squirmed under the older man's glare. When she finished speaking to him, John Hunt turned to Roberts, "We were just leaving, Mr. Roberts. If you have questions for my granddaughter in the future, I'll ask that you contact my legal team and they'll contact her at their earliest convenience to set up a meeting time that is mutually agreeable." Peter barely held back his snort of laughter at the look on Roberts' face. *Yeah SPAC, that's what a slap-down by a protective grandfather with the bucks to back it up sounds like.*

Jax flashed a quick hand signal to Peter letting him know they needed to move it quickly and Peter gave him a slight nod of understanding. "Come on, Lara, let's get a move on, we have another appointment and we don't want to be late." He was grateful she seemed to understand what he was doing and moved quickly toward the door. Just as they stepped around Roberts and his sidekick who had evidently been too insignificant to introduce, they were surround by members of their team and Peter noticed a couple of guys standing to the side that seemed to be scanning the area as well.

Kent leaned forward and quickly pointed out who they'd brought in, but one of the men Peter had noticed wasn't among those. "I see him, we're watching him as well. And unless he's got a whole lot of backup outside, we'll handle him quickly. I'd like to get you and Lara out of here and then a couple of us will introduce ourselves." The gleam in Kent's eye made Peter *almost* wish he could hang back and watch that for himself. He'd seen Jax and Kent's "introductions" before and they were usually pretty entertaining, but he wasn't about to give up protecting Lara just to watch his teammates beat information out of some flunky.

Peter had secured the key to the safe deposit box in his wallet and he was glad they'd electronically tagged it last night as a precaution. He was still trying to absorb the enormity of what they'd found in the box and he knew Lara was struggling as well. Fischer hadn't seemed as affected and Peter wondered about that as they settled in the back of the car. Without even being asked, Fischer took Lara's hand in his and said, "I know you all are shocked by what you saw in the box, but I can't really say the same. And if you think about it I think you'll understand why. Your parents have been in all the right locations to meet the kind of people who deal in untraceable currency. And while I'm not sure how they managed to accumulate so much and get it back in the U.S. without drawing suspicion to themselves, I can't say that I am surprised they managed it. Were there times when one of your parents would be gone for several days at a time?"

When Lara nodded, Fischer continued, "I'd be willing to bet those absences coincide with visits to the bank. The big question is, what did they do to earn it? I know Eric Roberts is determined to find out what's in the box and how it came to be there. And I'm sure his bosses are wondering how much of the chatter they're hearing is factual. I can read Roberts like a fucking book and he knows that even if they have no legal claim to the contents of the box, they'll hold it all until hell freezes over and all the while claiming its evidence." *And that, ladies and gentlemen, is why Kent and Kyle West are dying to hire my brother.*

Peter knew Fischer wasn't speaking hypothetically, he'd have heard every single thought Agent Roberts' had. Peter also knew Fischer's pause was to let Lara absorb what he'd said—not because he was finished.

After several long seconds, Fischer seemed satisfied Lara had taken in what he'd said and he continued, "According to Agent Roberts, your parents were working for the CIA and the agency knew full well about the payments they were receiving—what they don't know is how much money is actually involved and they'd like very much to get their hands on it but don't have a legitimate claim to it."

By the time they reached the penthouse Jax had already called to say they'd spoken with the man who had been watching and were satisfied they'd discouraged him from any further interest in Lara. Evidently the young man had shared a number of classes with her in college and when he'd seen her enter the bank he'd followed hoping for a chance to speak to her. It hadn't taken Micah Drake any time at all to verify the man's story and then Jax had sent him on his way. "Now we just have to deal with Eric Roberts. But I've spoken with John and he's making some calls, it seems my dad isn't the only one with contacts in the pentagon." Peter didn't even try to hold back his laughter, Jax had hated his father's connections when they'd been SEALs because his dad had kept very close tabs on his son—something their superiors found extremely annoying and they'd rarely missed an opportunity to complain about it.

"But I have to admit, I think John's plan is solid. If he can get Roberts reassigned based on his previous personal relationship with Lara, we'd be able to take advantage of the lag-time to move the contents of the box. And I'm in complete agreement that moving the goods is our best bet to flush out anybody who has an interest—and that includes Lara's parents because my gut tells me they are hiding rather than in danger."

Peter moved out on to the patio so they could speak privately, "I agree, but I'm damned mad about the danger they've put Lara in. We got lucky this morning that the young man you talked to was just a former classmate, but I don't think we have a prayer of flying under the radar unless we get Roberts reassigned or at the very least distracted enough about the prospect that we get the stuff out of there. And then we're still going to have to deal with whoever has been watching the bank—and my guess is there is a contact on the inside."

"Agreed and we're already working on it. That box has been rented for over twenty years so we know they have a contact inside the bank, and I'm betting it's one of the bank's long term employees so we're starting there." Jax paused briefly and even though he didn't need to tell Peter what he was thinking, he did, "I'm sure you're thinking the same thing everyone else is, the bank president is the obvious choice—but to be honest it's almost too easy."

"What did John have to say?"

Jax's laughter sounded through the phone, "John agreed, he claims the man wouldn't do anything he thought might hurt Elizabeth. Evidently the man is still carrying a torch for Lara's spirited granny." Peter didn't have any intention of following this conversation any further south, getting involved in Lara's grandparents' love triangle wasn't a place he was going to go—at least not willingly. "Okay, I'm assuming by the uncomfortable silence you are not interested in the rest of the story so I'm just going to say the bank president isn't alone at the top of our suspect list. We're going back to the suite, because our wives are feeling neglected. We'll meet at the club later and figure out what to do about securing those bonds— damn those things are far too liquid for my comfort."

Peter completely agreed, any piece of paper that could be converted into cash by anyone holding it needed to be in a safe place, hopefully John Hunt had a suggestion. After hanging up, Peter stepped back into the penthouse to the sound of flesh slapping flesh followed by a soft gasp. Stepping into the living room, he had to hold back his chuckle at the sight of Lara's very bare ass over Fischer's lap. Each cheek was sporting a single handprint so evidently he hadn't missed much of the action.

'Want to catch me up, brother?'

'*Miss Sassy here was determined to go to the club. She seems to think she needs to work. As if her fucking job would be in jeopardy if she missed a day or two because we want her safe.'*

Okay, his brother was obviously working himself up into a good mad—probably time to get involved. Even though he knew Fischer would never truly hurt her, that didn't mean Peter was entirely convinced either of them was thinking clearly at the moment.

'Two more swats then sit her up, I want to talk to her and you're angry.'

Peter saw Fischer stiffen just before his silent, *'Fuck!'* drifted through Peter's mind, letting him know his younger brother had come back from the edge. The last few days had been an emotional rollercoaster ride for all of them and this battle of wills really shouldn't be that much of a surprise.

Chapter Sixteen

Lara didn't know why she was pushing Fischer, but her mouth wasn't listening to her brain so she just kept digging herself deeper and deeper. By the time she found herself over his lap with her bare ass stinging, she was so emotionally overwrought it was a wonder she hadn't melted into a big pile of goo. She wanted to go to work and feel *normal* again. So much had happened in the past few days that she felt like she was constantly fighting just to stay afloat in the sea of churning emotions she'd been tossed into. And she was just tired of everything being out of control—even if she had to act out to do it, by God she was going to take a little bit of control back.

When Fischer lifted her off his lap and set her on her feet, Lara looked up to find Peter studying her. "Strip and kneel." Peter's command made her shiver even as she kicked her jeans and panties the rest of the way off and then removed her shirt and bra. Settling to her knees, Lara felt a strange sort of peace move over her.

This was familiar and settling, *here* she felt in control because even though she was handing over everything to her Masters, it was her choice. And putting herself in their hands let her relax for the first time in days. But there was still the niggling insecurity that they were only her Masters for the moment, Fischer had said they wanted her forever, but they still hadn't made any *real* commitment to her and it was becoming harder and harder for Lara to remain hopeful they would eventually collar her. And who would blame them for walking away? Hell, her life was spiraling out of control faster than she could pick up the pieces, let alone fit them back together.

She knew they were both watching her and the silence in the room was almost deafening. Lara just let her mind float while she waited for further instructions and it wasn't until she felt Fischer's fingers wrap softly around her wrist that she realized she'd been absently stroking her bare throat. "Baby?" *Oh craptastic. As if he wasn't already mad enough, I have just shown them both what a terrible sub I am. Yeah, just another reason for them to send me packing.*

FOR THE FIRST time, Fischer new exactly what was going through Lara's mind. It wasn't so much that he could hear her, but the combination of their prior friendship, his experience as a Dom, her unusually bratty behavior, and the unmistakable body language clue she'd just given them made her easy to read. When he'd wrapped his fingers around her wrist he'd felt her stiffen and then as her heartrate accelerated so did her anxiety. *Unfuckingbelievable. She still thinks we don't want her? How is that even possible? Fuck, I told her we planned to keep her.*

Fischer hadn't intended to broadcast his thoughts to his brother, but he hadn't made any effort to conceal them either. *'If you'd stop and think about it, you'd know the answer to that question.'* Peter's voice broke through his thoughts and it took everything Fischer had to not respond out loud. He could practically feel his brother rolling his eyes as he moved around the sofa and settled next to Fischer. "Tell us what you want, Lara. Stop hiding behind your fear and walk through it to get what you want." Fischer watched her eyes go glassy with unshed tears and he was afraid his brother was pushing her too hard.

Peter leaned forward putting his fingers under Lara's chin bringing it back up so they could see her face. "Don't hide—not from us and not from yourself. There is no right or wrong answer. There are not expectations other than the truth."

Fischer felt her pulse accelerate even more and watched her eyes dilate as her breathing quickened as well. "Baby, you're thinking too much. Stop trying to figure out what you are *supposed* to say or what you think we want to hear, because the only thing we want to hear is what's in your heart." When he felt her tremble he leaned closer, "How about if I ask you a couple of questions to get this started?" She nodded quickly and he felt his heart clench, knowing she was still so reluctant to tell them what she wanted from them told him exactly how poorly they'd handled the situation.

"You were a brat earlier and that is pretty unusual for you, can you tell us why you think that might have happened?"

He wanted to smile when she pulled in her bottom lip, chewing it silently as a wrinkle formed between her brows in concentration. "I remember thinking that I should just stop, I knew I was messing up, but I couldn't seem to stop. I just—I just needed something and I don't even know what. And even when I knew you were getting angry, I just kept pushing. And I didn't care that you were punishing me for it because I knew you would take care of me."

Fischer just nodded, he'd known she was pushing, but until Peter pointed it out, he hadn't know exactly why.

"You know there are rules and they are there for your benefit, right?" When she nodded, he continued, "And when you misbehave, you know there will be consequences—always. So by acting out, you were assured my attention and the comfort of something consistent because you haven't had much consistency the past few days, have you, baby?"

Her eyes went impossibly wide and realization lit up her eyes just before tears spilled over and she whispered an apology he didn't feel was necessary. Peter leaned forward and pressed a kiss to her forehead, "Precious girl, don't apologize for needing your Masters attention, but it might be easier on your backside if you found a better way to express that need." She nodded and shifted ever so slightly as if Peter's mention of the swats she'd gotten reminded her about her tender cheeks.

"Now, for the bigger issue here—you were rubbing your neck, any thoughts about why?" Fischer wasn't going to pussyfoot around, he was going to hit her with it straight and make her not only confront her needs, but express them as well.

He wasn't surprised when a fresh wave of tears began to fall. "I didn't even realize I was doing it until you grabbed my wrist." They let the silence between them build knowing she was hoping they'd bale her out and neither he nor Peter planned to let her hide behind her fear any longer.

Lara closed her eyes, and Peter's gentle, but demanding voice ordered her to open them so they could see her—hiding was simply not an option any longer. Fischer saw her take a deep breath and let it out in a rush before the words they'd been waiting to hear began to tumble out in a rapid stream of consciousness jumble. "I'm afraid you don't want me. No…that's not really it…I'm afraid you aren't going to keep me. I know you said you would, but…well, it's just that it was so easy for my parents to walk away, and if the people who are supposed to love you no matter what, are willing to leave…well, it's really arrogant of me to hope you'd want to stay. And besides, how can I ever hope to keep two gorgeous men satisfied for Pete's sake? Just look at me…I'm no model that's for sure. And you said you can't read me and I know that bugs you and you haven't ever said that you wanted to be committed to anyone so I don't know why I even hoped you would want to go there with me. But the more time I spend with you the harder it is to think about losing you and I can't even imagine working at Dark Desires and seeing you with someone else. I'm sure I'd just die a thousand deaths."

Fischer lifted her onto his lap and Peter at the other end of the short sofa pulled her small feet into his own lap. He gently pushed his thumbs in small circles at her arches making her moan and he felt her entire body relax. *"Mi amōre,* we've done you a huge disservice by letting you feel as if you're adrift.

"We certainly didn't mean for it to seem as if we didn't want you or that we were undecided about keeping you. What we *had* intended to do was to let you get focused on the trouble your parents have managed to get you embroiled in before we sat down and had this discussion—and not because our feelings for you are hinged on the outcome, but because we didn't want you to feel pressured." Fischer felt her shudder and knew the adrenaline that had driven her burst of openness was ebbing and the coming crash was probably going to be a big one. "All that being said, I for one still don't want to have this discussion right now. You are both mentally and physically spent, and even if you aren't of a mind to take care of yourself, we are."

Lara tucked her chin against her chest sighing and the defeated sound tore at his heart. She started to stand, but he and Peter both held her still. "I think I'd like to go rest for a bit and then I'll head out to my grandparents for a few days. This is why I should have kept quiet—damn my big mouth anyway."

Fischer felt his face contort with frustration but Peter's glare froze the words he'd been about to say right in his throat. How she could be so insecure when she was everything they'd always wanted was beyond confusing and starting to get damned annoying. "You'll go and rest, but then you'll be going with us to the club. Let us make something very clear—if you try to handle this situation on your own in any way, we'll tie you naked in front of the bar at the club and hand a paddle to each Dom who walks through the door. We'll let them each take a turn until we believe you have come to your senses, and then we'll fuck all the good sense right back out of you right then and there."

The ice-cold fear that pulsed through her was unmistakable. Peter had hit two of Lara's biggest hot buttons and Fischer didn't have a doubt in the world she would avoid that particular punishment like the plague. As a natural blonde, Lara's skin was always creamy white, but she'd actually paled even more at the thought of being so publically punished. What she didn't know was that neither he nor Peter were particularly fond of public scenes, preferring to keep what belonged to them out of the view of others. And they would never deliberately humiliate her. Oh, they'd push her boundaries—hell, Fischer knew it was their job as her Doms to push them, but humiliation wasn't their kink and it damned well wouldn't serve any purpose other than to send her screaming in the other direction.

Fischer pressed a kiss to her temple, "Cupcake, I want you with everything that I am—and I have since that first moment standing in the reception area of Dark Desires. And there are very few moments during the day that I'm not thinking about ways to get you naked and spread out for my pleasure. Believe me when I tell you, *me not wanting you* is the least of your worries." This time the shiver he felt move through her was all about arousal rather than fear, and he was probably more pleased than he should have been by that.

Standing with her still in his arms, he made his way down the hall to their bedroom as Peter followed. He really had planned to simply tuck her in for a nap, but when she pressed her lips to his neck and whispered, "I need you," all of his good intentions were melted by the flames of desire.

He and Peter both shed their clothes in record time after Fischer laid her on the edge of their bed. Peter moved down to her feet, once again pressing his thumbs against the arches of her feet, he told her to open for him and Fischer felt his own cock thump against his abdomen in response when her legs opened wide without hesitation. "Fucking beautiful. *Mi amōre*, your smooth pussy, all slick and swollen with desire is fucking gorgeous. I'll never get tired of this view, I can promise you that."

Fisher wouldn't have even needed to look, he'd have known the instant his brother's fingers slid through her wet folds just by watching the slight bowing of her back and the flush that quickly spread over her chest. Lara Emmons might be a trained submissive, but she was so responsive her body often reacted before her mind could regain control. Closing the gap between them, Fischer stroked her cheek with the back of his finger, the gesture was a silent demand for her to turn toward him and she didn't disappoint.

"Open for me, too, baby. I want to watch my cock disappear into that sweet mouth of yours. I want to watch it sliding between those beautiful red lips of yours as you take me time and again to the back of your throat." As she opened and he pressed forward, Fischer couldn't hold back his groan of satisfaction. "Holy fuck, every time I think it can't get any hotter, you prove me wrong." Peter was obviously upping the stakes and when she groaned in response to whatever diabolical tricks his brother's mouth was playing, Fischer worried he might come long before he wanted to. No woman had ever wreaked so much havoc with his control—Lara had completely bewitched him.

"She tastes exquisite. And I can tell when our woman is getting close to climaxing from the sweet taste of her honey, so you'd better remind her that she hasn't been given permission to come yet." Fischer had to grit his teeth to keep from reprimanding his damned brother for making Lara groan in frustration because the vibration had almost sent him over the edge.

'If you want in on the party you had better get inside her and fast. Holy hell she is taking me clear to the back of her throat and then swallowing—it's the sweetest kind of torture.' Peter didn't waste a second, he moved so fast Fischer barely had time to pull back before he grabbed Lara's ankles and yanked her quickly so her ass was nearly hanging off the bed and in one quick thrust, he was fully seated balls deep. Fischer took a quick step to the side and managed to slide back between Lara's lips just as she screamed at Peter's sudden intrusion. "Holy fucking hell, baby, you undo me!" He hadn't intended to come so quickly, but feeling her throat

muscles massaging his already over-sensitized cock was too much. "I'm coming, cupcake. Don't waste a drop of my gift to you."

Fischer felt the searing fire of his release shoot from deep in his balls before blasting from his cock in hot jets. The muscles of Lara's throat tightened around him pulling him deeper each time she swallowed and for a few seconds he thought his orgasm might never end. "Holy fucking Christ that was unbelievable. Thank you, baby, you are far too good at that." And wasn't that the understatement of the century? Hell, he'd gone over much sooner than he'd intended to, but he could tell by Peter's muffled curses he wasn't far behind.

PETER FELT THE first flutters of Lara's climax just before he gave her the command to come, knowing there was no way she'd be able to pull back after Fischer had come. He didn't want to punish her for coming without permission and damn it all to hell, he wasn't going to be able to hold out anyway. Peter slid his arms under her legs, hooking her knees over the bend of his elbows, changing the angle of penetration so the hard ridge of his cock head pressed against her G-spot with each thrust and Lara's gasp let him know just how much she'd appreciated the shift.

"Your responses feed my pleasure in a way I'd have never imagined possible, *mi amōre*. Come with me, let's go over the edge together." Before he could even take a breath Lara's muscles locked around his cock like a vise trying to pull him deeper into her body and he was lost. His vision actually blurred and darkened to the point he wasn't sure his legs were going to continue holding him up. He'd never had sex without a condom before Lara and he knew he never wanted to give up the intimacy of the skin-to-skin contact. Peter couldn't imagine a world without Lara in it—hell, he didn't even want to think about it.

Even in his sated state, Peter wanted to rage at the situation they'd found themselves embroiled in. Damn it all to hell, for a bunch of former Navy SEALs, they sure weren't making much progress finding Lara's parents. And as soon as they got her settled in to rest and his legs would carry him back down the hall, he planned to start making calls. Neither he nor Fischer wanted to move forward with the relationship until Lara was free to make decisions without being under the unnecessary stress of worrying about her parents. But he was getting damned tired of waiting and she obviously needed the security of knowing where they stood.

After cleaning up and settling their very drowsy, but sated sub in to rest, Peter stalked into their home office and hit the speed dial number on his phone assigned for Micah Drake. After a short conversation that told him abso-fucking-lutely nothing, Peter swiveled around in his chair to lean back and looked out the window behind his desk that looked out over the city. He didn't believe Lawrence and Rita Emmons were *missing*—it was far more likely they were hiding out, waiting for their daughter to remove the contents of the safe deposit box so they could step in and reclaim the contents. Peter knew Fischer felt obligated to give Lara's parents the benefit of the doubt—as the strongest empath in the family, Fischer had always been the most compassionate simply because he understood others' pain so well.

Thinking back on their childhood and how much

Fischer had struggled, until their parents had finally pulled their youngest son out of public school, Peter couldn't help but wonder how his younger brother had managed to hold out as long as he had. After that, their mother had homeschooled him, their grandmother had worked to help Fischer build shields to help protect him from the barrage of psychic energy he was exposed to in public places. Fischer had been able to attend private high school and college, but had known he couldn't follow his brother into the armed forces. Peter had not only understood, he'd encouraged his brother to follow another path—even though he was kept out of combat situations whenever possible, his exposure to intense emotions couldn't be completely avoided. As the least powerful empath in the family, Peter had known how much more his younger brother would suffer, and he'd spent a lot of time encouraging Fischer's pursuit of other ways to fulfill his need to help others.

Peter felt his brother enter the room before he heard him. "I'm not sure I ever thanked you for you that, you know. You saved my sanity and probably my life. I'm grateful for all the time and energy you spent encouraging me to find my passion." Fischer settled into the large leather chair behind his own desk and swiveled to face Peter. "And oddly enough, you were the only one who didn't seem surprised when I took the job Cam suddenly offered me, don't suppose you'd want to tell me why I got that offer?" Peter wanted to roll his eyes at Fischer's thinly veiled insinuation.

"We've been over this—a couple of times as I recall. I got you the interview, but you landed the job all on your own. Hell, you know Cam as well as anyone, do you really believe he's the type to hire a second-in-command as a favor?" Peter knew his brother had always felt as if he'd been "given" the job and then earned it later, but that simply wasn't the case. He might have asked Jax and Kyle to help Fischer get an interview, but his younger brother had earned the position he'd gotten.

"And I wasn't surprised that you were interested in working at a kink club because we'd shared women a few times and I knew how much you enjoyed it." And the more time Peter had spent with Kent and Kyle West after they'd married Tobi, the more interested he'd become in a polyamorous relationship. Jax and Micah's marriage to Gracie had also served as a motivator, and Peter smiled as he thought about the two women he now considered to be close friends.

Neither Tobi nor Gracie was a particularly well trained submissive—despite their husbands' best efforts. But both of them had big hearts and were loyal friends. And according to Fischer they'd both quickly befriended Lara when Cam and Cecelia Barnes first introduced them—hell, that alone would have earned the two sweet subs his favor. But the truth was, it was damned fun watching them run roughshod over his friends. Their combined military experience and records were nearly legendary and their reputations as sexual Dominants was almost as impressive. But when it came to their wives, all four men were putty—and Peter was nothing but envious.

Chapter Seventeen

FISCHER WANTED TO laugh as he listened to his brother's thoughts wander in an ever-widening arc. Peter might have started out thinking about Lara's case, but he'd quickly become distracted by the woman herself. It was not like Peter to be so unfocused, the challenges facing Lara had certainly derailed him. And her ability to shake him clearly showed how much different Lara was from the other women the two of them had shared—she was "the one" and Fischer was thrilled she affected Peter as much as she did him.

Peter and the others seemed to be ready to throw Lara's parents to the wolves for the danger they'd exposed their daughter to, but Fischer was withholding his judgement until he knew exactly what had taken place. His mind kept rewinding to a comment Lara had made when she'd seen her father's Bible in the box that had been delivered. She'd remarked that her dad would not have sent it unless he believed he wouldn't be coming back. It was her insistence that he wouldn't have willingly parted with it unless he'd been forced to, Fischer kept coming back to. *Forced? Or perhaps he was trying to send a message?*

"I think we should look through Lawrence Emmons' Bible again. I just can't stop thinking about it and that usually means I've missed something important." Fischer moved to the table where they'd left the things Mr. and

Mrs. Emmons had sent to their daughter. Picking up the black leather book, Fischer was almost knocked off his feet by the negative energy surrounding what should have been a book filled with hope and joy. "Did you touch this when it arrived?" Peter moved quickly to his side—no doubt having heard the shaking in his voice.

"No. One of the other's put everything in here and I haven't taken time to look through it. Why?" Fischer didn't bother answering, he simply held the book out for his brother and watched as his eyes widened in surprise when he set the small book in his palm. "Holy shit. There was some serious shit going down when this was packed up. See what you can get while I call Kyle, this changes everything." Fischer was grateful his brother's team already understood Peter's gift and respected it enough to take what he said seriously. So often people didn't accept what they couldn't see or feel themselves, so they didn't take warnings seriously—warnings that could have easily saved them a lot of trouble.

While Peter spoke with Kyle, Fischer took the Bible to the small sofa facing the fireplace at the other side of the office and focused his thoughts trying to center them on the book in his hands hoping to determine where Lawrence and Rita Emmons had been when they'd quickly packed the small box of valuables for their daughter. He hadn't realized he was speaking aloud until he heard Lara's soft voice relaying the information to Peter. When she started filling in the missing pieces of information, Fischer knew she'd figured out her parents' last known location.

"Bolivia," she said simply, "they were in Bolivia, I can tell by your description. I don't know why they were there...it's not even on the same continent as the location they'd given me, but considering what I've learned about them recently, I guess I shouldn't be surprised."

"Are you sure? Fischer's information was a little vague." Peter's comment didn't offend him because it was the truth—even as he'd been relaying what he felt, it hadn't seemed very clear.

"Yes, you described La Paz perfectly as well as the Yungas Road, also known as the Road of Death. That thirty-eight miles traverses some of the most spectacular scenery in the world, but it also claims almost three hundred lives every year. I had to make that trip twice and I can tell you I have never been more terrified in my entire life. But to be honest, it was your description of the Saler de Uyuni Salt Flats that convinced me." Fischer watched as her eyes became slightly unfocused as she let herself fall into what was obviously a far more pleasant memory.

"There is no place else like it, it's truly remarkable. Over four thousand square miles of salt flats and formations that make you feel as if you're no longer on earth. There are areas so perfectly flat after a rain it's like standing on a mirror your reflection is so crystal clear." Fischer watched as her eyes cleared and he saw her hesitance before she proceeded, "If they were left out there, there really is little chance they made it out alive. I've heard a lot of stories about condemned people being left out in the midst of the flats to die. It's not a pleasant way to go and I'm praying that isn't what happened to them." Pulling her into his arms, Fischer absorbed her shudder of fear before kissing the top of her sweetly scented hair.

"Why would they have been there? Any ideas?" Fischer hadn't directed his question to either Peter or Lara specifically and he wanted to laugh when they both answered at the same time.

"Lithium."

Peter gestured for Lara to continue, but she simply shook her head so his brother explained, "The Bolivian government has closely guarded their mineral reserves because their culture is so important to them, and they know other countries would exploit their vast resources. And since they are sitting on almost fifty percent of the world's lithium, they could easily call the shots setting up their own mining and refining facilities."

Lara nodded, "All of that is true, and since poverty and corruption are so closely linked it won't come as a surprise to find out governments are still trying to buy their way in. I don't know for sure, but I'd bet that is why we were *stationed* there several times over the years. I hate to think of that time in a negative context—because I have to tell you, Bolivia is one of the most amazing places I've ever been. The people are just as colorful as the goods they make, and the city of La Paz is breathtaking." '

Peter decided to give Micah a head's up, but planned to wait until they met with everyone at Dark Desires to let the rest of the team in on what they'd discovered. It didn't take them long to dress and get on the road and Fischer was glad the penthouse was close to the club. Within the hour they were all seated around the large table in the conference room and Lara was recounting every detail she could remember about their time in Bolivia.

Fischer was amazed at the wealth of knowledge among the team members and when they'd done a conference call with Jen McCall, he'd seen why the Wests' had recruited her. Jen's knowledge of the political climate in Central and South America was astonishing. Peter explained to both he and Lara that Jen had worked for the State Department and was stationed in Costa Rica for a time, but she'd been trained to work in several nations, Bolivia among them.

The instant rapport between Lara and Jen was a pleasure to see, and since he'd met Sam and Sage McCall when they'd been on Peter's SEAL team, he felt like he knew them as well.

The decision was made to wait for Micah Drake to work his computer magic before making any moves to find her parents. Fischer knew Lara wasn't expecting anything good to come of their research and after hearing Jen McCall's description of the political climate in the area, he was inclined to agree. The chances of the Emmons escaping the area—if their real purpose for being there was uncovered—was practically nonexistent. Unfortunately, they'd also need to confer with Eric Roberts because it was technically still an ongoing investigation. Sighing to himself, Fischer didn't want the man anywhere near Lara, he'd had his chance and blown it hurting her deeply in the process. But the bigger issue was, Fischer had heard the man's thoughts and knew how much he regretted what had happened between them—and he knew how much Roberts wanted a second chance.

WATCHING FISCHER ESCORT Lara out of the room was torture. Peter could almost see the waves of sadness coming from her, hell, they reminded him far too much of the waves of heat shimmering over the streets during the heat of summer—and they were about as discouraging. Once she was out of ear shot, Jen spoke quietly, "I have to tell you, this is a clusterfuck in the making guys. You can't go all commando and waltz into Bolivia demanding answers. They'll just drop you over the edge of some mountain highway and be done with it. They are protecting billions of dollars and people are killed every day for far less."

Peter listened as various members of the team expressed their agreement before Jen zeroed in on him, "If the Emmons were left out in the Saler de Uyuni Salt Flats, their only option would be to make the one hundred plus mile trek across the Atacama high desert. Keep in mind that is one of the driest places on earth. It's a brutal area and there aren't a lot of seaports that would offer the type of transportation the Emmons would need to escape. But that does gives us another place to look. The government of Peru is more cooperative so if they made it to the coast, we'll probably be able to track them."

Jen paused for a moment and Peter could almost hear her internal battle. Without being physically close to her, she was very difficult to read and it was also obvious the little imp had learned some blocking tricks from her friends at Prairie Winds. This time when Jen started speaking, her voice was filled with compassion, "I think Lara already sees how this is likely going to end, but the very worst thing you can do is risk your lives to prove her right." He must have looked puzzled because she smiled, "The risk is twofold. First of all, I'd be *very* worried about anyone going into this area right now—it's a hot spot. You and I both know the CIA doesn't have agents in the area just for grins and giggles, between the Bolivian's lithium reserves and the sodium nitrate cache in the Atacama, the place is a warmongers wet dream. The CIA wants to monitor who's interested in all those wonderful explosive components and they aren't particularly interested in helping the Bolivians. You would probably end up facing a fate similar to the Emmons' and Lara doesn't need to lose you, too."

"Okay, you said it was a two-fold issue, what's your

other point?" Peter wasn't saying he completely agreed with Jen, but she had made some valid points. It seemed foolish to endanger the men on the Prairie Winds' team just to prove the obvious. And if the Emmons worked for Uncle Sam, let the damned CIA go in and pull their people out.

"Well, more importantly, if we don't send a team in there, she'll get to hold onto her hope—and right now that's all she has left. Let it fade slowly over time, it will be far less painful that way, if you know what I mean." This time, Jen's advice made perfect sense, but he would have assumed the opposite if he'd had to guess. Maybe it was just him, but not knowing would make him crazy. When she laughed he realized he'd been shaking his head. "Don't you shake your head at me, Peter Weston, and I don't need to be an empath to know what you're thinking. Sure, for a Dom, not *knowing* is tantamount to not being in control, but there are times when not knowing is a reprieve—it means you have time to process a loss over time rather than when you are feeling the most vulnerable."

After saying their goodbyes, Peter looked around the table and saw nothing but compassion from his teammates. Nobody said anything for several seconds, and it was Kyle West who finally broke the silence, "If any of you repeat this I swear I'll fire your ass—no questions asked—but what Jen said makes sense and I wouldn't have thought about it. If you stop thinking like a soldier and a Dom, it's easier to see." Shaking his head at the blank looks he was getting around the table, he finally rolled his eyes, "Jesus, Joseph, and Mary, you guys, try to see this from your woman's point of view. I'll tell you what, how about I get my mom to explain it to you all?" Peter swore every man at the table, including Kent, paled.

Lilly West was a force of nature that no Special Forces operative in the world would take on willingly. Hell, she'd blown up a boat on the river behind the club awhile back with a rifle shot that took out the motor before ripping into the explosives on board. She'd been the one to make sure her sons met Tobi and the two women were as close as any mother and daughter Peter had ever seen. Lilly also had a complete lock on the whole spine of steel southern woman personality even though her heart was pure gold, and nobody Peter knew would willingly cross her.

Once Kyle had issued the challenge of bringing in Lilly, the conversation had quickly returned to Jen's points and they'd all agreed to table the discussion until they knew more about what they were facing. And Kyle reluctantly agreed to face off with Eric Roberts since leaving it to Peter seemed like taking the short road to needing bail money.

By the time Peter made his way down to the club's main room, the edgier members of Dark Desires were out in full force and there was an undercurrent of energy so tightly strung he found himself wondering if he wasn't projecting his own tension onto those around him. Kent stepped up beside him and asked, "Is it just me or do you get the sense this crowd is a lot more on-the-cusp than our membership at Prairie Winds?"

Kyle stepped up to them shaking his head, "I was down here late last night and a couple of the scenes scared the hell out of me, and I didn't even think *that* was possible at this point. I think it's safe to say Cam was far more comfortable with the darker side of BDSM than what we have at Prairie Winds." Peter had been working at Dark Desires for several months and he still wasn't at ease with it, and he doubted he ever would be.

Peter and Fischer had already been talking to the Wests

about tightening up the screening process during membership renewals, hopefully they'd be able to shift the climate of the club environment in a more moderate direction going into the future. Peter knew the changes they hoped to see wouldn't happen overnight and it would likely cost them a few of their long-term members. But everyone agreed the changes to the overall vibe of the club would eventually make it more comfortable for kinksters from a wider range of age groups. One of the things members of Prairie Winds repeatedly noted as a selling point was the mentorship opportunities they found in the more diverse membership at Prairie Winds. The younger members appreciated the chance to learn from those who had been in the lifestyle for decades and older members enjoyed helping others find the sexual fulfillment that had often been missing from their lives.

Kyle leaned forward trying to keep his voice from carrying despite the pounding music pulsing from large speakers mounted around the room. "The contents of the safe deposit box have been moved." Peter must have looked surprised because Kyle laughed, "And that look is exactly why we did the switch so quickly, we knew no one would be expecting it."

Kent snorted a laugh, "Yeah, and nobody paid a bit of attention to a middle-aged granny wearing orthopedic shoes carrying a monster handbag waltzing into the bank to put new 'goodies' into her 'safe box' either. Well, she didn't go unnoticed—it's more like she flew in screeching like a banshee right under their radar."

"Tobi?"

"Oh yeah, and she had a great time with that little escapade too, we're going to have a hell of a time keeping her out of team meetings now." Kyle rolled his eyes and laughed. Everyone on the Prairie Winds team knew how badly Tobi West wanted to be included, but she wasn't a trained soldier and neither of her husbands had any intention of letting her out of their sight long enough for her to actually work an op. The work they did as contract operatives was dangerous—often involving covert infiltration into depths of hell no one should be exposed to. And if there was one thing Tobi West was not—it was covert. The petite but curvy blonde was a firecracker—she'd be a far better distraction than operator.

LARA LOOKED UP just in time to brace herself as Tobi West barreled into her. For such a petite woman Tobi was a steamroller with a rib crushing hug, but it always made Lara smile. "Hey, girlfriend, I didn't think you were ever going to get here."

"I know, both of my Masters were already here, but Barfing Barbie held us up." Lara looked up to see Gracie slowly making her way toward them.

"Does she actually look sort of green or is it just me?" Lara had always wanted children someday, but she might need to rethink that plan if this was the way things went.

"Well, I can tell by that 'scared spitless' look on your face I should probably lie, but some rat-fink bast...ille would just tell my Masters and then I'd get spanked—hmmm come to think of it, that sounds like a mighty fine plan." Lara laughed as Tobi seemed to be having a conversation with herself about whether or not to lie about something that was already frighteningly obvious.

Gracie stepped up and nudged Tobi aside, "Move your blooming ass, loaded person has the right of way." God

Lara loved these two women and their antics were just what she'd needed.

Tobi moved over and shook her head, "Good grief, she drove a truck for some farmer for extra money almost ten years ago and learned that nonsense…and I'm still hearing it, where's the justice in *that*?" This time Lara laughed out loud, which earned her more than one glare from nearby Doms. Tobi leaned close and whispered, "Damn, girl, keep it down or I won't have time to gossip before our Doms show up acting all incensed at our lack of decorum." Rolling her eyes in typical Tobi West fashion, she giggled and bounced from foot to foot. "I got to play dress up today and work an op—oh dangling Dalmatian doodads, I really do like saying that. *Worked an op*—yep, that sounds wicked."

"Oh for cripes sake, just tell her because I see our Doms stomping this way. Damn the grapevine in a kink club is faster than the speed of light, I swear NASA really needs to sit up and take note."

Lara listened as Tobi rattled off how she'd gone in to the bank and cleaned out the safe deposit box, turning everything over to Lara's grandfather who had planned to secure the contents out of Eric Roberts' reach. Tobi had rattled the story off quickly, but not fast enough.

"Kitten? What did I tell you about speaking publically about Prairie Winds business? I swear you couldn't keep a secret if your life depended on it."

"I most certainly can keep a secret—I do it all the time. I haven't said a single thing about your mom's blood pressure." Kyle spun Tobi around so she was facing him so quickly Lara wondered if her friend was dizzy. "Shizzle. See what you made me do? Boy, oh boy, Lilly is gonna be pissed at me and it's all your fault."

"Be careful, my love, because you are jumping into the deep end here."

Lara watched as Kyle deliberately stepped closer to Tobi so when she unconsciously took a step back her shoulders rested against Kent West's black leather vest. "And you've tied a lot of weight around your pretty little neck, sweetness. Might want to spill it because my brother and I can be ruthless when we want information." Even from the side, Lara saw a shiver race up Tobi's spine just before the corners of her mouth turned up and Kyle scowled at her.

"I don't know what just went through your mind, Tobi West, but you'd better think about it very carefully. Consider where you are and who you are with—do you really want to push both of your Doms? The owners of this club? The men whose reputation you will be tarnishing if you don't behave?" Kyle's voice had gotten softer as he'd been speaking and the quieter he spoke the more threatening he sounded.

This time it was Lara who shivered just before strong arms wrapped around her from behind. Peter's lips pressed just below her ear before he mused, "Tobi is fine, don't worry. This is a game they play often, they all three love the challenge and I assure you they keep very close tabs on their mother as do their fathers. Lilly and Tobi are a lot alike in that regard—it takes a village to keep them in line." Lara felt herself relax and watched as Tobi seemed to consider her options.

Finally, heaving a big sigh before batting her lashes up at Kyle, Tobi seemed to concede defeat, "Okay, I guess I can't keep a secret. But pickle pucker this morning was the most fun I've had in ages and I couldn't wait to share with my besties."

When Tobi fluttered her lashes at Kyle again, Lara heard his frustrated growl, "It's a good thing I adore you more than life itself, because you are absolutely incorrigible. Now let's go find an empty St. Andrew's Cross, maybe between us, my brother and I can flog the information about our mother out of you." Tobi squeaked when Kyle leaned forward and picked her up over his shoulder. The move flipped her short skirt up baring her ass to the room and when she squirmed he gave her a solid swat, "Quiet, wench, or I'll set you back down and strip you before escorting you all over the club while Master Kent and I decide on the perfect location for our scene."

Watching the three of them walk away, Lara found herself hoping she'd find what Tobi and Gracie had with their men—she wanted it to be with Fischer and Peter, but she wasn't about to jinx it by assuming things would work out for the three of them. Her family had put her in a such a tenuous position everyone around her felt obligated to help her, and while she appreciated it—their relationship didn't feel *real* to her. Looking over at Gracie, Lara couldn't hold back her smile seeing the way Jax and Micah watched her so closely. Gracie might grumble about them "hovering" but it was easy to see how she practically glowed in their presence.

Gracie managed to maneuver herself until the two of them were standing together in a small corner near the bar, "You can have it too you know?" Lara knew she'd been lost in her own thoughts, and now she was scrambling to figure out what she'd missed. Gracie laughed, "Lordy, I do so love that panicky look on your face when you're trying desperately to figure out some comment Tobi or I have picked up out in left field." Lara wanted to laugh at Gracie's strange take on American expressions, but she let it go. "I meant you could have what Tobi and I have with our men. Peter and Fischer look at you the same way our husbands look at us, except maybe there is more longing there because they don't know if you're on board with the idea or not." When Gracie turned toward her, Lara saw a new side of her friend, "Don't lead them on if you aren't serious, because they're in love with you and it's already going to be hard enough for them to let you go—don't keep them on the string if you aren't in it for the long haul."

Lara gasped in surprise, not only was she shocked Gracie thought she'd do something so callous. But more importantly, the Central American beauty she considered a friend was usually quite perceptive, so it staggered Lara's imagination how Gracie had gotten the situation so misconstrued. "I think you might have things a bit confused, Gracie. And while I'm grateful you think I'm worthy of them, I think you should know it's not me who is holding back."

Gracie met her gaze head on and shook her head, "But it is. Don't you see? They are just waiting for you to be ready to accept what they have to offer. It's all in your hands—the submissive always has the ultimate power in any D/s relationship. Peter and Fischer Weston are Dominants, there is no doubt about that—*none*! But they are also honorable and believe in the guiding tenants of our lifestyle. Safe, sane, and consensual will override their personal desires. And with all the challenges you're facing they don't want you to make a decision you might later regret."

"How do you know this?" Lara hadn't intended the question to sound as sharp as it had come out, and she smiled hoping to soften the sting she saw when Gracie arched a dark brow in question. "I'm sorry, I don't want to seem rude, but I really am interested in where this is coming from. They've told me that we'll discuss it later and that they want me, but to be honest there wasn't much conviction in it." Try as she might, Lara wasn't able to keep tears from filling her eyes and found herself blinking quickly to keep them from spilling over.

Everything about Gracie's demeanor softened as she reached forward and pulled Lara into a hug, "Oh, honey, they are holding back because that's what they think you need. I think you are stuck in that frog pond thing and they are trying to make sure you don't do anything while you're so stressed out." *Frog pond? I really need Tobi here to interpret for me.* Lara fought the nervous giggle she felt bubbling up because the one truth of the entire mess was the fact that her life was indeed becoming almost unrecognizable. And looking back she could see it all started when Simon Ericson sat down at her table. Even though she felt foolish for falling for the line he'd fed her, she couldn't manage any real anger because he'd been doing his job and there was still a small part of her that thought he had actually liked her.

Jax McDonald's deep voice came from behind Gracie and Lara couldn't help but return his smile, "*Cariño*, I believe your frog pond reference might be confusing Lara a bit. Perhaps you are referring to the frog in a pot of water that slowly comes to a boil? The fact the frog doesn't realize he's in trouble until it is too late?"

"Oh. Well, close enough." Gracie gave a dismissive wave of her hand and Lara found herself laughing out loud. She'd learned early in their friendship that even though Gracie's English was excellent, the intricacies of culture were often difficult for her to navigate. And the fact she was so blasé about it made it all the more amusing in Lara's view.

The six of them moved to a small sitting area so they could watch the Wests scene. Jax and Micah settled Gracie between them on the loveseat, but not before she'd gotten a couple of swats for trying to kneel in front of them. Lara had covered her snort of laughter at Gracie's grumbling with a cough and avoided her own punishment even though neither of her Masters hadn't looked convinced by the innocent look she'd given them.

Before she knelt between their two chairs, Peter turned her so she was facing him while Fischer placed a large pillow on the wooden floor between them. Pulling her close, Peter tapped the inside of her thigh and Lara immediately obeyed the unspoken order to widen her stance. "Good girl. Now, let's see if we can't set the mood for what you're about to see." Lara felt the brush of Fischer's fingers at the back of her neck and before she realized what he'd done, the sides of the halter-top she wore fell to her waist. Anticipating her reaction, Peter had encircled her wrists and held her arms at her sides.

"Leave your arms down, precious girl. We want to enjoy the view and show you off a bit in the process." Turning to where Jax and Micah sat with Gracie, Peter's voice was already becoming rough with lust, "Beautiful, isn't she? Such amazing breasts, soft pink nipples that turn the most incredible shade of rose after she comes."

In her peripheral vision, Lara saw Micah nod as he answered, "She is beautiful, and I do believe you two will be able to cure her of that little shyness problem that seems to be an issue. Let's see if we can't help." Looking down at Gracie, he gave her a grin that was almost predatory. "Lose that pretty top, baby. I do believe your other Master has a couple of pretty clamps in his pocket and I'm anxious to see how they look framing your pretty nipples."

Lara felt her own nipples draw up tighter as Gracie pushed open the buttons at the front of her shit without even hesitating. She saw Gracie's head tip back and heard her groan of pleasure when her Master grasped the tip and squeezed. When Peter's mouth closed over her peaked nipple, Lara felt her head fall back just as Gracie's had as she lost herself in the sensation. When her legs started to shake and her knees almost folded out from under her, Lara felt the vibration of Peter's chuckle before his diabolical fingers pinched her other nipple, rolling it tightly between the pads of his fingers. He leaned back just enough that his words sent a wash of warm air over the wet peak causing it to draw up so tightly she swayed on her feet, "That's it, let us take you there, *mi amōre*." Before Peter even finished speaking Fischer had slipped the clamp on to her nipple and quickly tightened it just enough that she'd whimpered at the sharp pinch. The second clamp was in place before Lara even realized they'd moved and her mind hadn't even registered the fact she'd closed her eyes until she heard Peter's command to look at him.

She was already feeling dazed from the flood of all those happy little hormones racing through her blood, but the look of raw desire in Peter Weston's eyes pulled her so close to the edge that for a few seconds, she worried she might actually come from his look alone. Fischer whispered over her shoulder, "Bend over and spread your legs a bit more." She didn't mean to hesitate, but it took his words a couple of seconds to register and she heard him growl behind her, "Your hesitation just cost you your skirt, cupcake."

Lara's mind was swinging like a pendulum between

embarrassment and need, but she responded to the sound of her skirt being ripped from her body and immediately slid her feet apart and bent over. The move put her nose to nose with Peter who gave her a look so hungry she had to blink to be sure it was real. Fischer's hand pressed at the small of her back and Lara instinctively arched into his touch, causing her bare ass to thrust out, which then she felt a cool wash of air move over the slick folds of her pussy.

"Jesus, Joseph, and sweet mother Mary, you are so fucking gorgeous, baby." She didn't have any time to respond before Peter pulled her forward the last inch and pressed his lips against hers. The kiss started out tender but quickly escalated as his hand cupped the back of her head, his fingers threading through her hair to tilt her face to the side to deepen the kiss. Peter's tongue danced along her bottom lip and then, just as he plunged forward, Fischer pressed something round deep into her slick channel.

The only thing Lara could liken the moment to was the overwhelming feeling of sensory overload she'd had the first time her grandparents had taken her to the symphony. She'd felt the vibration of the kettle drums all the way to the souls of her feet, the trill of the woodwinds had sent goose bumps up and down her young arms, and the string section reminded her of rolling ocean waves.

Lara remembered how she had been completely bowled over trying to separate all the different instruments until she'd finally just let go and enjoyed the totality of the moment—she tried to let that same sense of surrender move through her again. The small stones dangling from the nipple clamps she wore swung back and forth adding a new layer of intensity to the pinch while Peter's tongue was plundering her mouth in a kiss so scorching she felt the fire all the way down her spine, and knowing Fischer had likely just inserted a vibrating egg into her core was the icing on the cake.

Feeling the first tremors of release starting to build she fought against it and knew she was losing the battle, but Fischer's sharp slap to her ass brought her back from the edge. Peter let her pull back from the kiss, just enough that he could press his forehead against her. "You need to make a decision, Lara, and here are your choices. One, Fischer removes his belt and lays three stripes over your sweet ass right here in front of everybody so that as you kneel and watch the Wests' scene you'll be continually reminded of how you allowed fear to overcome your desire. Or choice two, you agree that you belong to us and that even though we have a few details to work out, you are agreeing to wear the collar I have in my pocket for you."

Fischer knelt to her side, his tongue circled the outer shell of her ear before he spoke, "This collar is simple, but it's still an outward symbol of an internal commitment made by all three of us, baby. We've been working with a designer on your permanent collar, but it isn't quite finished yet." Lara's mind was spinning as she tried to take it all in, but one thing stood out from all the confusion—she wanted them with every fiber of her being, and she wanted to belong to them forever.

Without hesitation she simply said, "Two." Lara was sure she hadn't even gotten the word all the way out before the entire room burst into applause. No sooner had she blinked than she found herself kneeling on the stage where the Wests had been just moments before. When everything finally came into focus, Lara realized she knelt on a large deep purple cushion and there were buckets of beautiful flowers surrounding them. Tobi and Gracie were standing at the edge of the stage and both women gave her a thumb's up before their Doms' glares had them lowering their hands.

Still trying to get her mind wrapped around everything that had happened in the last few minutes, the only thing that remained clear was that she'd made the right choice. She hadn't let her fear override her bone deep desire to reach out and grasp what she wanted. Gracie's little pep talk had done exactly what her sneaky friend had intended it to—it had make Lara realize how simple it was if she'd just open her mind up to the possibility that not all men walked away at the drop of a hat.

It saddened her to think she'd let the actions of one man have such a huge negative influence. She'd never experienced heartbreak before Simon Ericson walked away without ever looking back. Well, this time it was her turn to walk away from him—or at least from the damage he'd done to her heart. And the simple truth was, she'd probably used the experience to hide from her feelings because he really had been as honest with her as he could. Sighing to herself, she let all the sadness and fear melt away when she looked down at the gold chain coiled in Peter's upturned palm. She couldn't hold back her smile when she saw the small charm that would lay atop the hollow at the base of her throat. The small golden cupcake was engraved with the words 'Mi Amōre', Lara was overwhelmed with emotion and felt the first tears slide down her cheeks. The fact they'd combined their pet names for her as a reminder she belonged to them, touched her more than she would ever be able to explain.

She watched as Peter turned the charm over to reveal a small hole in the back. "The key goes here. Fischer and I each have one, and we'll wear them around our neck on a chain that matches yours so there is a piece of your collar over our hearts at all times. When your permanent collar is ready, we'll schedule a formal ceremony and replace this set with the one we plan to wear for the rest of our lives."

Lara was barely able to hold back her sob, but the fresh rush of tears gave away her emotion. Fischer reached forward and brushed the tears away, "I sure hope those are happy tears, baby." When she simply nodded, he smiled, "Good to know." And then looking at his brother, he added, "Let's collar our sweet sub so we can suffer through a few toasts before getting the hell out of here, because I for one can't hardly wait to fuck our sweet sub."

The soft snick of the lock closing was the sweetest sound Lara had ever heard and she had about two seconds to enjoy it before Tobi's and Gracie's voices filled the air. She'd barely even gotten to kiss her Masters before her two friends wrapped her in a short robe made of fabric so sheer she wasn't sure why they'd bothered. The next half hour was filled with congratulations and so many toasts Lara was grateful she'd followed Tobi's advice and opted for ginger ale.

Peter or Fischer kept a hand on her at all times and Lara was surprised at how much comfort she found in their touch. For the first time, she realized how much more emotionally settled she felt when they were physically close, as if something in them settled the storms that often churned in her mind. Those storms had been why she'd gotten several undergraduate degrees without ever moving on to advanced placement programs even when she'd wanted to. Even her former boss, Cameron Barnes, had spoken to her about it when he hired her as a nanny for his daughter—a job she'd been paid for, but never gotten to do before he moved his family to the Caribbean. He'd reviewed her employment file and challenged her lack of focus and direction. Lara had always sensed the restlessness in herself, but she'd never been able to find a solution—until now.

Chapter Eighteen

Four Months Later

PETER LISTENED AS Eric Roberts spoke to the members of the Prairie Winds team gathered in one of the smaller conference rooms of Houston's FBI headquarters. The building was large enough to allow team members to enter from several different directions, which helped disguise the fact they were meeting on-site. Anytime members of a team that was supposed to be covert gathered in one place the threat of exposure became an issue, so using different entrances and staggering their arrivals was a necessary inconvenience. Kyle West had told him on the way downtown the powers-that-be had been less than thrilled to host the CIA's *tête à tête*. They'd finally relented in light of the fact there were rumors floating around that Lara was being watched, and being John Hunt's granddaughter had no doubt provided them with an added incentive. Kyle had laughed as he'd recounted how the local feds had changed their tune when the oilman's name came up in the discussion.

The past four months had been filled with a lot of changes at Dark Desires, keeping everyone distracted enough to push the concerns about Lara's parents onto the back burner. Yesterday's phone call setting up today's meeting had definitely unsettled Lara and Peter hated seeing the peace she'd finally found in the past few weeks fade so quickly from her pretty blue eyes. She'd been invited to today's meeting but had opted to spend the morning riding with her grandfather instead. He wasn't sure if she was avoiding the man she'd known as Simon Ericson or bad news, but he and Fischer had agreed she shouldn't have to attend the meeting if it made her uncomfortable to do so.

Neither he nor Fischer had been particularly thrilled with the prospect of Lara being near Roberts either, but their reservations were far different from hers. He and Fischer had both heard the man's silent, but heartfelt regrets. And they both knew better to tempt fate by giving him a second chance. No—he'd fucked up his chance and she'd paid a hefty price for his lack of consideration so Special Agent Roberts wasn't going to get another opportunity to hurt her.

Lara was rebuilding her relationship with her grandparents and personally, he was thrilled she was finally finding the balance she'd needed for so long. He and his brothers had a close relationship with their grandparents, so they understood the value of her relationship with John and Elizabeth Hunt.

Peter thought back on the times he'd bounced ideas off his grandparents and how often he'd found it easier to talk to them than his own parents. When he'd made that observation one afternoon while walking along the beach with his grandfather, the old man had laughed and assured him that grandparenting was a far better "gig" than parenting.

Their sweet woman had been spending quite a lot of time at their estate and Peter enjoyed watching her blossom as her self-confidence grew. John Hunt's staff had assessed the contents of the safe deposit box and the estimates had been staggering. Lara had been unimpressed and she was working with her grandmother to set up a foundation to benefit several local charities.

Peter knew Lara wasn't interested in the actual size of the trust fund her grandparents set up for her, and anytime someone mentioned it, she simply waved them off. Hell, if he hadn't already been in love with her, Lara's complete disregard for personal wealth would have drawn him to her like a magnet. The rare times she'd seemed to care about money were those when she was giving it away. He chuckled to himself when he thought about her phone call to CeCe Barnes, the two of them had brainstormed ways the money could be used to benefit crippled children in Cecelia's U.S. and Caribbean clinics. Lara was excited about finding ways to use the money—their little sub had the soul as pure as any he'd ever known.

After half-ass listening to Agent Roberts while thinking about Lara, Peter finally zeroed in on the man's words, "We have witnesses that are sure they saw the Emmons boarding a small fishing boat in Arica Chile three months ago." *Three months ago?* If that was true, they'd had plenty of time to contact Lara. "We've also heard some chatter coming out of several of the countries the Emmons were working in—seems we aren't the only ones looking for them."

Kyle leaned forward to look over the papers Roberts slid over, "Looks to me like they better hope your team finds them first. Christ, they've managed to paint some pretty big targets on themselves."

"And their daughter," Peter practically growled as he skimmed the documents Kyle had slid down to him.

Roberts took a deep breath and looked over at Peter,

"Look, let's just clear the air here, okay? I know you don't like me and quite frankly I don't blame you. Hell, when it comes to Lara Emmons, *I* don't even like myself." Peter respected the fact Roberts was being up front with him but didn't respond because it was obvious the man had more to say. "I know I don't have a prayer of rekindling what Lara and I had, but I really did like her, and I'd like to be her friend. One of the things I've learned over the years in this business is that you can't ever have too many friends." Sighing deeply, Roberts seemed to take a several seconds to consider his next words, "Listen, I know the diamonds and bonds we've been looking for were stashed in a safe deposit box, I know where, and I know who cleaned the box out." Smiling, Roberts let his gaze drift over to the West brothers. "Tell Tobi the disguise was great, but her perfume gave her away. I don't know what that stuff costs you, but it's worth every cent."

Peter and the others laughed as Kent and Kyle both cursed under their breath. "The point is, I haven't shared that information and I'm not planning to. Hell, the plans Lara and Cecelia have for that money far exceeds anything our government would do with it. Anyway, I don't want either of your women in trouble. We've have a good working relationship and I don't want to fuck it up. I have put the word out that the Emmons stiffed their daughter and that she's as pissed as anyone about their duplicity." Roberts sat in the large leather chair at the end of the table and looked directly at Peter, "The bottom line is, I'm doing what I can from a distance to make up for hurting her, and I'd really appreciate it if you and your brother would ease up a little and at least let me apologize to Lara. She deserves that much from me, and for what's it is worth, you're a couple of lucky bastards."

The rest of the meeting was productive as they shared the intelligence they'd gathered and Peter wasn't surprised to learn Micah Drake had discovered various homes the Emmons had purchased around the world. So far they hadn't been spotted at any of those properties, but no one was betting against it since there were renovations being done to two of the more remote locations. The contractors insisted the changes had been slated and paid for well in advance so the only thing they could do now was sit back and wait.

LARA LOVED THE feel of the wind blowing through her hair as her mare ran the track in front of her grandparents' home. She'd forgotten how much she'd relished the freedom of horseback riding and hated the fact she'd let her mom and dad color her opinion of the two people who had never been anything but loving and supportive. She'd lost too many years with her grandparents and she was determined to spend as much time with them now as she could. Despite the fact she'd been young when the split had occurred, she still should have known better than to not at least *listen* to both sides.

Neither her grandmother, nor her grandfather expressed any bitterness, and that only made her love them more. She and her grandfather had brushed their mounts, laughing when she'd slipped and fallen directly under the beautiful mare she was planning to ride. The gentle horse had given her a look she could have sworn was just shy of an eye roll.

Lara hadn't been paying attention to where her grandfather was on the track as they'd exercised their horses, because they had deliberately spaced themselves apart to keep the horses from giving in to their natural inclination to race. When she suddenly noticed her grandfather standing alongside the large gelding he'd been riding at the gate she was approaching, she quickly pulled up on the reins. Lara had heard people who'd experienced traumatic events say they felt as if the world had both slowed down and sped up at the same time, but she'd never understood what they meant until that moment. She heard what sounded like firecrackers going off a split second before her horse reared up as chunks of turf popped up from the track just a few feet in front of her, reminding her of corn popping in a hot skillet.

In the next beat of her heart, she realized she was sailing through the air and to her horror, she watched helplessly as her grandfather grabbed his thigh and slid to the ground, blood seeping through his fingers. She'd been so focused on her grandfather, Lara hadn't prepared herself for the jolt of hitting the ground. The jarring impact of landing flat on her back knocked the air from her lungs and she lay there gasping for breath. Shouts filled the air around her and all she could think about was getting to her grandfather, and wondering if anyone else had noticed how pretty the sky was. *Why can't I breathe? Those white clouds look just like cotton on blue silk. I have to get to Gramps, he was bleeding. Why did someone set off firecrackers around the horses? Don't they know how dangerous that it? I must have fallen asleep. It's getting dark out here. I'll just rest for a minute and then check on him. Who am I supposed to check on?*

FISCHER HAD BEEN sitting on what Elizabeth Hunt referred

to as the front veranda sipping sweet tea with his vivacious hostess when he heard the unmistakable sound of gunfire. Without even thinking he opened the mind link he shared with his brothers and let everything he was seeing and hearing flow out freely. Distance was ordinarily a huge hindrance when they wanted to communicate telepathically, but he was hoping the surge of emotion would be enough to overcome the problem. He'd never felt more helpless in his entire life than he did as he closed the distance between himself and the track. Watching John Hunt sink out of sight and Lara fly off the back of the horse she'd been riding turned his blood to ice.

Seeing a horse stand on its hind legs, front legs pumping in the air had always seemed like poetry in motion—until it was the horse the woman he loved had been riding. As she disappeared behind the tall rail fence, Fischer noticed her gaze was fixed on her grandfather and she didn't seem to be making any attempt to cushion her own fall. The moment his hands connected with the top wooden rail of the fence, he heard two more shots from the trees along the drive leading to the house, but the second set of gunfire hadn't sounded the same. He could only hope that didn't mean there were two shooters.

Fischer was sure he'd never forget the sound of Lara's body hitting the ground and the whoosh of air leaving her lungs. Leaning over her as she gasped for breath, he remembered the terror he'd felt the first time he'd had the wind knocked out of him. There was a part of Fischer's mind that registered both Peter's and Adam's alarm just as his phone vibrated in his front chest pocket. Knowing it would be Adam, he pulled it out hitting the speaker button and simply shouted his location and hung up. Fischer knew his oldest brother would alert the authorities if they hadn't already been called—Peter knew where he was and wouldn't have needed to call and ask.

Lara's eyes were unfocused and the minute he touched her, Fischer felt her slipping into the dark void of unconsciousness. The relaxation the darkness would bring would help her breath easier, but since he hadn't seen her land, he worried about the implications if she had a concussion. It quickly became apparent he wasn't the only one there watching Lara, but he was grateful the two men who were obviously agents didn't hesitate to step in and help. They'd stopped the bleeding in John Hunt's upper leg before Fischer heard the wail of sirens quickly closing in. Keeping his attention on Lara, he felt her begin to stir and he placed his hand on her shoulder when she tried to sit up.

"Stay where you are, baby, let's be sure you don't have any back or neck injuries before you begin moving around." Seeing her eyes fill with tears she tried to blink back squeezed his heart. "I know you are worried about your grandfather, but I assure you he is fine. We obviously had more company than we knew about and they've been taking very good care of him. The paramedics are here now and they'll get you both loaded up in just a few minutes." Fischer leaned over her and kissed away the tears that ran from the corners of her bright blue eyes, "Don't cry, cupcake. He's fine and we'll figure this all out. The horses are being taken care of and you can bet your sweet ass my brother is tearing up everything in his path trying to get to you."

John Hunt's heart rate had spiked so the EMTs wanted him transported quickly even though it had returned to normal after he'd been told Lara had regained consciousness. The second ambulance arrived just as Fischer heard the distinctive *thump, thump* of a helicopter. Before the paramedics made their way to Lara, Peter was sprinting the distance between where Lara lay on the soft turf of the track and the grassy center of the large oval where the FBI's helicopter had landed. *'Glad you were meeting in a place with blades, bro.'*

'This tells you how eager they were to get rid of us. How is she?'

Fischer didn't get a chance to answer before his phone vibrated for the second time and he knew better than to ignore Adam again. Stepping away to take the call, Fischer let Peter take over while he filled their older brother in on what had happened. Adam was well connected and would be able to ensure they had the full cooperation of local law enforcement and he promised to send a couple of his own security to the hospital to help keep Lara and her grandfather safe until they could figure out who had been responsible for their injuries. Smiling to himself as he hung up the phone, Fischer wondered if he'd ever outgrow the comfort he found in talking to his brothers. Knowing both he and Peter had their family's support and blessing in making Lara their own was just another assurance they'd made the right decision.

An hour later they were still standing alongside Lara's bed waiting for the doctor to see her when Peter's thoughts filled his mind, *'I'm fucking fed up with this. I'll be right back, I'm going to make a couple of calls and see if we can't light a fire under somebody's ass.'* Fischer nodded and held Lara's hand as Peter explained that he'd be right back and stepped quietly from the small room. She turned to him and grinned, "He's calling somebody to hurry this place up, isn't he?" He would have laughed if he hadn't been so surprised. "You aren't the only one who pays attention you know? I watch you both too, and I can tell when you have reached the end of your patience. It saves my ass—literally, being able to know when I'm getting close to that line and these folks raced by that point about forty-five minutes ago."

Fischer didn't even try to hold back his laugh, "Cupcake, you are amazing and you are also right. I'd expect to see a doctor in just a few minutes, and knowing my family I wouldn't be surprised to see the Chief of Staff walk through the door." He could see the skepticism in her eyes and worked hard to hold back his grin when the door opened moments later and a man introducing himself as the hospital's chief neurologist walked in. Peter followed with a self-satisfied expression that was easy to read.

Two hours later, after Lara had spoken with her grandfather, they were on their way back to the penthouse. John Hunt had assured his granddaughter that he planned to milk the fourteen stitches he'd gotten for all they were worth and would have her grandmother waiting on him hand and foot in no time at all. They could all hear Elizabeth's protests in the background and Fischer was thrilled the elderly man had managed to make his granddaughter laugh despite how stressful their day had been. Once she'd disconnected her call, Lara leaned against him and within seconds he heard her breathing even out and knew she was sound asleep.

'We'll get an update from Kyle and Kent as soon as we get her settled, but it doesn't sound like the kid they caught knows much.'

Chapter Nineteen

Kyle West was straight up pissed. Eric Roberts had his nose so far up the ass of Lara Emmons' case Kyle knew the man had to be skating on thin ice professionally since the man was seriously stretching the bounds of his jurisdiction. The interrogation of the young man they'd detained in the trees had been short and sweet since he didn't know jack shit. He was a financially strapped college student working at a local gun range who'd been promised an absurd amount of money to fire two shots into the dirt causing a distraction. The kid didn't know the identity of the woman who'd hired him and all of their communication had been done over the phone. And the kid seemed to be truly mortified that two people had been hurt as a result of his greed and carelessness.

Looking at his laptop screen, Kyle shook his head when Peter had asked what charges the shooter was facing. When his friend's jaw dropped, Kent spoke up, "Listen up, this was John Hunt's call. And, well—frankly, I hope like hell I'm as wise as he is someday."

Kyle shook his head, "Not in this lifetime and probably not the next." Then turning his attention to Peter and Fischer, he continued, "Something about the kid's interview impressed John Hunt's attorney, who then talked to Hunt. The young man has been offered the opportunity to have all traces of this incident expunged from his record in exchange for his compliance with a rather rigid list of requirements, including public service hours, completing college with a GPA above a 3.0, and he'll be living in the Hunt's guest house, working his ass off for the next two years."

"Christ, is he planning to adopt the damned kid, too?" Kyle could tell Peter wasn't entirely thrilled with what he was hearing, but Kyle was equally sure Lara was going to be thrilled when she heard what her grandfather had done.

"Can't say as it would surprise me much." Kyle laughed and shook his head, "Elizabeth grilled her husband for almost an hour before signing off on the plan. Hell, the kid wants to be a SEAL someday and I suspect BUDs is going to seem like a cakewalk after she gets done with him."

Kent leaned into the frame of their call and added, "I can tell you two aren't thrilled with this plan, but I want you to know everybody who has talked to this kid agrees this is a great idea. He's really bright, but dirt ass poor—and if he isn't set on the right path now, we'll be dealing with his brilliance later after the wrong side of the law has a chance to fully train him, and quite frankly we've already got enough of those folks out there."

PETER FINALLY LET out a breath, he'd never had trouble trusting his former teammates but when they were talking about the woman he loved—well, he was finding it a much harder sell. Fischer didn't appear to be any more pleased than he was, but he appeared to be resigned to accepting what had obviously already been set into play.

Kyle leaned forward and the move got both Peter and

Fischer's attention, "Here's the kicker. The distraction worked—someone entered the horse barn during the chaos in front of the house. The board that had recently been replaced was removed and the fake key we left there was taken." This was the shit Kyle West lived for and the smile on the man's face reflected just how much he was enjoying the way things were working out. Hell, Peter wouldn't be surprised if Kyle didn't start rubbing his hands together in glee doing his best Snidely Whiplash imitation. "We have people in place waiting for them to show up at the bank. But let's face it, Lawrence and Rita Emmons have been spooks for a long time, so I'd be awfully surprised if they boldly walked into our set up."

"There isn't much we can do aside from watch, because they haven't broken any laws as far as anyone knows." Kent shrugged and then added, "I'm sure their employers are interested in how they've managed to accumulate such an impressive *portfolio of assets*, but I don't think they've got anything to pin on them."

Peter finally gave in and asked the question that had weighed on his mind from the beginning, "Which of them is really the leader here? I know the natural assumption is that it's Lara's dad, but for some reason I have the sense that's wrong."

"I think the general consensus is that Rita is the push behind everything. Lawrence might be the brains, but it's his wife who is driven and, her profile indicates she is far more aggressive than her husband who easily slid into his missionary persona. Rita, on the other hand, struggled with living the simple life, thus their lavish vacations several times a year." Kyle's explanation made sense and Peter assumed that was a large part of the reason they were never in one location for more than a few months.

"Now, we need to switch directions before our lovely wife bounces herself right out of the 'fuck me' shoes she showed up in a few minutes ago."

"Doesn't she know those four inch heels aren't going to make any difference? She's never going to be tall enough to be a threat." Peter laughed out loud because he could hear Tobi gasp in the background.

"Peter, I swear I don't know why my friend thinks you hung the moon. Now, Fischer is a sweetie, but you are just mean. Does your mama know you're mean to girls?" The little imp was wound for sound, damn he missed working at Prairie Winds.

Fischer nudged him aside and flashed a smile at Tobi that had been getting him girls' panties since he'd been a damned teenager, "Darlin', both of my older brothers are beasts, and our mama tells me that she was determined to keep trying until she got it right. That's why I'm the youngest." *Oh spare me. 'Honestly, Fischer, you keep flirting with the Wests' woman and they'll take you apart at the seams.'*

'Ehhh, she and I are just playing with you so lighten up. Jesus, you are such a tight ass. And the plans she's made for our proposal and collaring are fucking amazing. This is my way of thanking her. She'll get punished tonight for playing with me, and she and her Doms will all be thanking me—watch and see.' Peter wasn't entirely convinced, but decided he wanted to crawl into bed and cuddle with Lara more than he wanted to argue with his brother so he let it go.

Tobi had made all the arrangements they'd discussed and even added a couple of details they might have overlooked and Peter wished the woman wasn't in Austin because he'd have loved to thank her in person. Kent and Kyle had flown back home as soon as they'd known Lara and her grandfather were alright, and Peter could tell the three of them were also getting antsy to end the call. Kyle assured them there were people watching the bank, but it was anybody's guess how long the Emmons would wait to make a move—personally, Peter was betting months.

The party was just a few days away, and so far they all believed Lara still hadn't gotten wind of their plans. Their sweet sub knew they were treating her to a spa day with Tobi before taking her to Topper's for dinner. She'd been looking forward to visiting the lavish restaurant owned by a member of the club because the small venue's reputation among those in the kink community was well known. Peter and Fischer loved hearing her gush about what the subs in the club had told her, because what she'd heard was pretty tame considering what they'd seen during their visits over the years. They'd never taken a sub there, but they had been invited guests on several occasions and Peter could hardly wait to enjoy the experience with the soft, naked woman currently sleeping peacefully in their bed.

LARA LOOKED DOWN at the dress and shoes the staff at the spa had spread over the small bench in the enormous dressing room and felt her pussy moisten just thinking about her Doms taking her to Topper's. She and Tobi had spent the entire day at the spa. They'd been waxed, washed, buffed, polished, and styled to perfection. When she realized she was standing in the middle of the room with Tobi, and they were both stark naked, Lara couldn't hold back her giggle.

"Just realized you're naked and *comfortable,* didn't you? Hell, girlfriend, we've been naked most of the day. We hit the front door and the first thing Mistress Scarlet said to us was 'Strip.' Damn it to donuts, I thought we were at Dark Desires for a minute."

"I know. A few months ago I would have been completely freaked out about anyone seeing me naked."

"Yep, totally understand. And don't forget I was laying on the table right beside you as the technicians ripped hot wax off every square inch of our pussies and asses, so I think it's safe to say neither one of us have any secrets left. And no offense, but that's as intimate as I think either of us ought to plan on getting." And wasn't *that* the understatement of the day? Because as open and nonjudgmental as she was, Lara had never been sexually attracted to women.

The spa their Doms had chosen was owned and personally overseen by the strictest Domme at the club. Lara had seen Mistress Scarlet reduce male and female subs to tears with just a look—she was a total stickler for protocol, and Lara still panicked just thinking about being on her radar. She had been more accommodating today, but she'd also made it clear there would be no room for negotiating.

"I still can't believe they gave her permission to paddle us if we gave her any grief. And frickin' frack, I can't say that I particularly enjoyed that *cleanse* either." Tobi's pout made Lara giggle even though she really had tried to hold it back since she wasn't sure her friend had completely forgiven her for escaping that particular part of the day's activities.

Knowing Scarlet was following very specific instructions from their Doms had made her commands easier to follow. And the fact the statuesque redhead had shown them the text from Kyle giving her permission to deal with any 'issues' in any manner she chose, had gone a long way in guaranteeing their cooperation. Lara had been careful to avoid any confrontations all day and thought she was home free until the lovely Mistress stepped into the room, gave them a smile that definitely didn't meet her eyes, and simply said, "Come with me."

When Lara looked around for a robe, the Domme shook her head and gestured for them to follow. "You won't need a robe, we aren't going far and I've made sure no one else has access to this area." She glanced at them over her shoulder and chuckled, "Your Doms were very specific about who could and who could not see their property. They are a possessive group, I'll say that for them." When they stepped into a room that looked too much like a doctor's office for Lara's comfort, she came to such an abrupt stop Tobi plowed into her from behind.

"Damn, girlfriend, your brake lights don't work for shit. Oh, sorry, Mistress." Tobi was continually in trouble for cursing and Lara almost laughed out loud when the Domme grinned.

"And you were so close, too." She laughed, "Although I'm not sure either of your men would have believed me if I'd told them you'd gone the entire day without cursing. They seemed convinced you'd rack up some points for them to play with this evening." She pulled on a pair of latex gloves and gestured toward what looked like a narrow metal table with a black leather padded top. "You first, Tobi. Lean over and spread your legs nice and wide. Your Doms left a couple of things for you. And by the way, that cleanse you disliked so much? You're going to be grateful for that later—I promise you."

Lara watched as Tobi stepped to the bench and positioned herself just as she'd been directed. "Good girl. You really are lovely, it's a pity your Masters don't share with anyone besides each other." Lara watched as Mistress Scarlet covered the tip of the plunger she'd picked up from the small tray on top of a chest of drawers with a large dollop of lube and then the scent of oranges filled the air. "Okay, reach back and spread those sweet cheeks for me, let's get you all softened up so you're ready for their gift." Lara watched as the Domme gently inserted the tip of the plunger and slowly pushed the lube into Tobi's ass. Her touch hadn't been anything but clinical, but it was obvious Tobi's body was responding to being dominated because her pussy was glistening with her arousal.

Mistress Scarlet had obviously noticed Tobi's embarrassment, because she'd laid her hand on Tobi's lower back in a comforting gesture as she reached for a fairly small butt plug. "This isn't a large plug, but it has some rather unique features. I'll leave the explanation to your Masters, but I'd advise you to be careful—you do *not* want to lose this little jewel. It probably set your men back at least a grand." *Holy shit, a thousand dollars for something to stick up somebody's ass? That's just wrong.*

The words had no sooner gone through Lara's mind than Tobi muttered almost the exact same thing. Mistress Scarlet didn't miss a beat, she gave Tobi two quick swats to each ass cheek. Tobi's complexion was as fair as Lara's and her ass cheeks blushed a deep pink almost immediately. "Damn, your skin is amazing. It's no wonder the Wests are totally taken with you. Now, stand up slowly. Move over by the other table—you can hold Lara's hand while I take care of her."

Oh hell, no. That sounded downright terrifying and Lara took an involuntary step back and even she realized she'd gasped—the sound bounced around the small room amplifying her fear. When she looked over at the other tray, Lara felt as if ice had suddenly replaced her blood. The joy she'd been feeling just a few minutes earlier had evaporated into pure terror. The strange metal circle with a smaller circle inside seemed to be connected to a chain but with the small black dots filling her vision, Lara was entirely sure she was seeing clearly.

She could hear female voices, but they sounded far away and oddly distorted as if the sound was traveling through water. Lara finally realized Tobi was standing right in front of her shouting, "Breathe," and she managed to suck in a large gulping breath. Tobi looked over at Mistress Scarlet who actually looked concerned and asked, "Can you please tell her that you aren't going to hurt her. I know what that is, but she doesn't and it's scaring the bezeesus out of her."

Surprisingly, the usually unflappable Domme nodded and moved to the tray. She briefly explained how the device would be fit over Lara's clit, keeping the hood back and allowing the sensitive nub to feel even the smallest movement of air or the lightest brush of fabric. Lara realized her gaze was riveted to the tray and the only thing she could utter was "chains."

The Domme seemed to snap out of her worry and grinned, "There are other pieces and they are all chained to one another, so a small movement in one area will quickly cause a domino effect of stimulation. I can assure you they have spared no expense either, this little set up is remarkable. Now, get up on the table and lay back. Tobi will be allowed to hold your hand and hopefully we'll be able to avoid any more problems."

Table? The one with the straps and stirrups and the fucking spotlight that'll probably give my 'personals' a sunburn? That table? Lara was frozen in fear, her feet felt like they'd been fitted with concrete boots, and it didn't matter that her brain was screaming at her to move—her legs just wouldn't cooperate. She didn't realize she'd spoken out loud until Tobi and Mistress Scarlet both burst out laughing. Lara gapped at the woman—damn, she didn't think she had ever even seen the intimidating woman smile, let alone laugh.

"Oh for heaven's sake. Stop looking at me like I just sprouted another head. I laugh sometimes. There really is a woman under the Mistress Scarlet persona, you know." Lara just stared, her mouth gapping open in stunned disbelief. "Maybe it would make you feel better to know that I am also a Registered Nurse. I only work part time now that the spa is doing so well, but I'm fairly confident I can fit you with these pieces without causing you any permanent harm."

Lara actually felt the blood drain from her face before the Mistress turned to Tobi and shrugged, "Damn, she really can't take a joke at all, can she?" When she turned back to Lara, the change in Scarlet's expression completely disarmed her. "Listen, there isn't anything on this tray that is going to hurt you. Each piece is designed to bring you nothing but pleasure, even though I have to admit you may get so wound up before they let you come you'll swear it's painful." Patting the black leather pad on top of the table, Scarlet's tone shifted subtly, "Come on now, let's get this done. My phone just vibrated in my pocket and that means your men are coming up from the parking garage. You don't want to ruin your evening by starting out being punished."

Chapter Twenty

Lara had to focus on putting one foot in front of the other just to walk down the hallway. On a good day she was challenged to walk in heels, but with her clit exposed to every brush of the silky fabric of her dress and her nipples were so sensitized, keeping her shoulders back was becoming almost impossible. She'd never seen clamps like the ones the evil spa owner has put on her. The inner and outer rings were placed over her nipples and the rings were spread apart pinching the nipple from all sides at the same time. The dress she'd thought was so silky soft a half hour ago now felt like sandpaper as it flowed over and around her breasts.

The nipple rings had chains that went over both her shoulders and down her abdomen. Those that graced her shoulders would look like glittering straps for her dress to the casual observer but they fell down her back and were fastened to the fine chain encircling her waist. The pretty golden chains highlighted the golden threads in the fabric and she'd quickly discovered their dainty design was deceptive. They kept her from slouching forward to relieve the tension on the chains in the front that connected the nipple rings to the ring holding back the hood of her clit.

Lara felt Tobi's hand on her elbow when she wobbled and turned to her friend, "I can do this…I can. As long as I stand perfectly straight and don't breathe, I'll be fine."

When she started to laugh at her own absurd words, the sharp tugs on her nipples and clit made her gasp. "Oh sweet baby Jesus. Note to self—no laughing."

"Oh brother, your Masters are really pushing you. I'm sorry about asking about those balls too by the way. I wasn't trying to remind her about them, sometimes my mouth gets ahead of my brain."

"Don't worry about it, I'm fairly sure she hadn't really forgotten them. She was just distracting me by tossing you under the bus. Every time I move those damn things bump against each other and it's like have a tuning fork stuck up your cha-cha while the maestro tunes up the orchestra." When Tobi burst out laughing, Lara wrapped her arms around herself desperately trying to keep from laughing. "No...stop, please. Your laugh is contagious and you're torturing me." Of course the harder they tried to stop the harder they laughed until they were both leaning against the wall gasping for breath.

"Damn and double damn, I haven't laughed that hard in ages. I'm glad you aren't angry with me for being a blabbermouth, because the truth of it is—I'm probably not going to get better anytime soon." And then, pulling Lara gently back to the center of the hall, Tobi started to lead her toward the door to the reception room.

Lara was surprised to see Mistress Scarlet standing in the open doorway smiling at them. "Are you two okay?" Lara was relieved to see the other woman's coy smile. "I wasn't sure exactly how to help, and honestly I was enjoying the show too much to interfere."

"Yes, I think we're going to make it, but it was touch and go for a while. Thanks for everything—I think." Tobi's grin was pure mischief and Lara had to bite the inside of her cheek to hold back her laughter.

The minute she stepped through the door Fischer wrapped his arms around her and pulled her against his chest. Lara pressed her face against the side of his neck and moaned, and hoped her soaking pussy didn't begin leaking down her legs. "Baby, you smell absolutely delicious. And that was before the scent of your sweet honey made its way to me."

Peter pressed himself against her back and leaned down to pull her earlobe between his teeth biting down lightly. "Do you like our gifts, *mi amõre?*" The pressure of his chest pressing against the chains snaking down her back pulled the nipple rings upward and Lara didn't even try to hold back her moan. Her entire body was lighting up with arousal and she felt a new rush of moisture to her sex.

Both men stepped away from her at the same time and Lara shuddered at the loss of their warmth. Lara blinked up at Fischer, warmed by his indulgent smile. Looking around, she was surprised to see Tobi and her men had already left. "Come on, cupcake, we need to get going or we won't make our reservation." Taking his hand she let him lead her out the door, every step upped her arousal until she felt her knees begin to tremble.

Peter noticed her distress and stopped her on the sidewalk, studying her intently. *'Damn, Scarlet has those chains so tight she is going to come before we even get to the fucking car. And how the hell is she going to sit down?'*

'I warned you the woman is a straight up sadist at times. The fact she's a nurse still scares the hell out of me.'

"Lara, it's obvious to us that Mistress Scarlet has misjudged the tension required for our gifts to you to be beneficial—rather than devastating." Peter's last words were said under his breath and Lara didn't think he'd actually intended to say them out loud. She didn't even try to respond because by this point her breathing was little more than quick pants as she tried desperately to not move a single muscle. "You have two choices." Lara tried to focus on his words, but the roar of blood rushing through her ears blocked out most of the words. Her body was on fire and there wasn't a chance in hell she could make any decision beyond whether or not to take another breath.

FISCHER COULDN'T HEAR Lara's thoughts, but as long as he kept his hands on her smooth skin he could feel the turmoil boiling close to the surface. He cursed himself for allowing Scarlet to put the clamps on Lara. But the chances of them ever getting to Topper's if they'd done it themselves was somewhere between slim and none. "Brother, I don't think she can make a choice right now. There's a security camera to our left. Let's turn her and you block our driver's view and I'll see what I can do to help her out. Once they'd gotten her into position, Fischer pulled the front of her dress down one side at a time lengthening the chains and he also released some of the tension around her tortured nipples. Cursing under his breath, he leaned forward and pressed a kiss against her forehead.

"I'm sorry, cupcake. That wasn't at all the way we wanted this to go. We'll check the clit ring once we're settled in the car." Looking over to where the limo sat idling nearby, Lara didn't care they'd forgone their usual Towne Car—she was just grateful. She gasped as she slid over the soft leather seat, the friction on her exposed clit was almost enough to send her over the edge. The stainless steel balls deep in her channel vibrated as they bumped together when she stopped moving and she moaned as her pussy began pulsing in response. Chuckling, Fischer grinned over at her, "Now *that* reaction is much more of what we had in mind."

"I still think we need to check the clit clip, I'm sure the Mistress of Mayhem is torturing what isn't hers to torture. Lean back against Fischer, *mi amōre,* and let me check." Ordinarily, Lara would have been embarrassed to tears at the thought of displaying herself so wantonly in the back of a car, but desperate times called for desperate measures as her grandmother was fond of saying. His muttered curses caused puffs of air to move over the exposed bundle of nerves ratcheting up her desire until her hips jerked up in a silent plea for more. Her body was working on pure adrenaline and reflex, and the moment Peter's warm fingers gently brushed the side of her clit, Lara exploded.

Fischer had been ready, sealing his lips over hers catching her scream and there was a small part of her brain that registered Peter's tongue lapping at her sex as he hummed his approval. "Fucking gorgeous. The appetizer of the Gods. And as usual, my big brother has been served first." Lara opened her eyes slowly and was relieved to see the soft smile on Fischer's face, grateful he wasn't angry with her for coming without permission. Looking down, she realized her dress was back in place and the pinch around her clit wasn't nearly as intense. She knew the ring was still holding back the little ruby's protective hood, but it no longer felt like it was being held by a pair of pliers. Fischer obviously noticed her bewildered look and laughed, "Baby, you went off like a rocket. We had time to make the *adjustments* that needed to be made while you were still in orbit."

Peter let his hand rest on the top curve of Lara's gorgeous ass, pressing his palm over the dimples he knew graced her lower back. He loved tracing those small indentions with his tongue and feeling her shiver in response. The glass-enclosed elevator that whisked them up to Topper's was dimly lit with golden light that made her blond hair shimmer like the halo she deserved. How their sweet angel had endured those chains tugging on her pretty pink nipples was a mystery to him. They wouldn't ever let another Dom or Domme touch their woman again—lesson learned.

The clit ring had been far too tight and if Peter had his way, Mistress Scarlet would be taking their class for Dominants again in the very near future. Flexing his fingers, Peter was thrilled when Lara leaned into his touch. After piecing together bits of information and getting to know her over the past few months, it had been easy to understand why Lara had been incredibly self-conscious and shied away from physical contact with anyone she didn't know well. Years of moving and living in places where her blond hair and blue eyes made her an obvious target had taken their toll. But she'd blossomed into a confident woman and they were pleased they rarely saw glimpses of those old fears when she was overly tired or stressed.

Leaning down, he brushed his lips against her ear, "Do you like the way the balls caress the walls of your vagina, baby? They're partially filled with oil so the movement of the liquid amplifies the vibration. I've seen Doms sit back and watch while their subs danced with those little jewels inside, and I assure you the dancing becomes seductive very quickly."

"And if it doesn't, there are other ways to amp things up a bit." Peter knew Lara hadn't fully understood Fischer's comment, but she would—soon. Walking through the restaurant, Peter smiled at the other patrons—most of whom were in place specifically at their request. The reservation list for the exclusive dinner club was months long and Peter didn't want to know how many favors had been called in to make tonight possible.

"There are a lot of club members here, is that because the owner is a member?"

'Just an observant little sub, we should have known she would notice.'

'Yeah, she doesn't miss a trick. God, I'm thrilled we're finally proposing to her. I want her to be ours in every way.' Peter couldn't have agreed with Fischer more. Pulling out her chair, he pulled up the back of her dress and pressed the chair against her knees so she was forced to sit. When she tried to look around making sure no one had seen her, he smiled. "Remember, Lara, this club is owned by a man who is very much into our lifestyle, and everyone around you is as well; and they all know you belong to us. Now, spread those lovely legs and hook your ankles around the outside of the chair legs." When she complied, he leaned over and kissed her cheek, "Good girl. Now hold very still and be quiet while we pour your wine."

Their table had already been set and the wine waiting for them so it didn't take long to hand her a small glass. He smiled at the way her fingers trembled, looking over at Fischer he nodded for his brother to continue. The table was clear glass, another nod to Topper's kinky clientele—subs weren't allowed to hide their bodies from their

Masters' view just because they were eating dinner. "Cupcake, pull your dress up so we can see that pretty bare pussy. We want to see what belongs to us and we want you to see the pretty jewels we added while you were drifting back to earth a few minutes ago."

The surprised look on her face almost made Peter laugh out loud. When she hesitated, Fischer simply raised his brow and her shaking fingers immediately inched her dress up until the faceted diamonds Peter had attached to the clit ring caught the golden flickers of candlelight sparkling against her pink flesh. "Good girl. Perfect in fact, being able to see those tiny jewels laying against the wet lips of your sex, knowing you are wet for us—well, *mi amõre,* that is *about* as perfect as life gets." Peter hadn't missed the way she tensed at his emphasis of 'about', but he wasn't about to give away their secret too soon.

As they enjoyed their dinner, Peter or Fischer made sure one of them was touching her at all times. Their bond was growing and both of them loved the fact they were finally able to read her most of the time if they were skin to skin. Once she forgot about the fact her sex was visible to anyone walking up to their table, she relaxed and seemed to enjoy her dinner. They limited her wine intake because they wanted her head clear when they got to the club—the decisions she'd be making this evening would affect all of them—forever.

Chapter Twenty-One

LARA SAT IN the back of the limo staring at the enormous diamond and sapphire engagement ring on her left hand and thought how it had gotten there. She'd watched in stunned silence as the two of them had adjusted the hem of her dress and then slowly turned her chair until she could see they'd attracted the attention of every other person in the dining room. When they'd each knelt in front of her and Peter had opened the small black velvet box he'd pulled from his pocket, she'd started to cry. She couldn't believe they actually wanted to make her their wife, and she'd barely squeaked out, "Yes" before the entire room erupted in applause. They'd been surrounded by well-wishers and the congratulations had continued until they'd finally made their way to the elevator.

Now looking over at Peter, she was surprised to see him watching her closely while stroking his cock. When he knew he had her attention he quickly ordered her to kneel in front of him. "While you suck me, your other Master is going to prepare you for the second half of this evening's festivities. Spread your legs nice and wide. Perfect, now arch your back and show him that pretty ass of yours."

"Oh, and what a lovely ass it is. I'm going to tell you what I'm doing, my lovely bride-to-be, because this is a very special day and I don't want it ruined by fear." Lara opened her mouth and skipped all the preliminaries, pushing her mouth over Peter's cock until the tip was pressed against the back of her throat in one quick move.

"Holy fuck. I swear on everything holy, your mouth is fucking lethal." She didn't need to see him to know he'd leaned his head back and closed his eyes, she recognized the tone of his voice and knew exactly how he was reacting. Pleasure ran through her in a sharp spike, knowing she could make him moan her name filled her heart with pure joy. They gave her so much pleasure and so rarely took their own until she'd come multiple times, she was thrilled to have the chance to give first.

She felt Fischer's finger massaging lube into the ring of muscles around her rear hole and moaned around Peter's cock—the vibration earning her another moan as his fingers threaded through her hair tugging gently. "Not yet. I want to savor this moment. Put your left hand up on my thigh, *mi amōre*. I want to admire our ring on your finger. Damn, I can hardly wait until we are married."

Lara moved her left hand to his thigh and her heart swelled as his fingers traced the boundaries of her ring. She didn't want a huge church wedding and she knew Peter and Fischer were going to push for sooner rather than later. But she doubted their mother or her grandmother were going to let the two men deny them the pleasure of planning a wedding. All thoughts of white lace and roses were pushed right out of her mind when Fischer removed his finger from her ass, causing her to wiggle her ass seeking his attention, he laughed, "Greedy little sub. Patience is a virtue, baby. I'm just getting the next piece of your gift. This very interesting looking piece of plastic is designed to stimulate all those sensitive nerves at the opening of your anus. Most of the pleasure associated with anal sex—at least from your point of view, is centered right there. This little gadget is going to make you feel all that pleasure anytime we want you too because it's remote controlled."

The only warning she had before she felt the first vibrations was a soft click as he turned the device on. At first it felt more like tingling pulses encircling her most private opening, but holy mother of God her entire body responded in a fraction of a second. Her reaction was so intense Lara felt as if every muscle in her body had clenched at the exact same moment. Her sex flooded with moisture and she felt droplets racing down the insides of her thighs. Fischer pressed kisses to her lower back murmuring words she couldn't make out because her mind was far too fragmented to comprehend anything other than pure pleasure. Nothing existed in that moment but the electrical storm raging in her body.

WATCHING LARA'S HIPS flex and her back arch when he switched on the stimulating ring sent so much blood to Fischer's already throbbing cock he was almost lightheaded. He knew his brother was just seconds from coming and he wanted Lara to go over at the same time so he pulled the mall remote from his pocket and hit two buttons at the same time. There was no way she could hold out against the increased stimulation around her ass and the vibrating balls deep in her channel. They hadn't turned the balls on before now because the natural movement of her body provided had been enough to keep her on edge, but he wanted to send her into orbit now, so he turned them on as well.

Lara stiffened and screamed around Peter's cock and

Fischer watched as his brother's eyes rolled back in his head as he shouted his own release. As an empath, Fischer fought to buffer the sensations his brother was feeling or he'd have come in his pants like a hormone-crazed teenager. Watching Lara's throat move as she swallowed Peter's release was one of the most erotic things he'd ever witnessed. And the flush of her skin as her body convulsed in orgasm was beyond beautiful. Fischer turned off both devices as Peter pulled their sweet woman against his chest. "You undo me. You are everything my brother and I ever dreamed of finding, and you've agreed to marry us. I'm not sure I've ever been this happy."

Fischer and Peter helped Lara move back on to the seat after he'd washed and gently patted dry her sensitive pussy. He was glad she hadn't been able to see his stupid grin as he'd moved the soft warm cloth down the insides of her thighs. He'd been ridiculously thrilled they'd aroused her to the point it was evidenced in a sweet trail to her knees. Handing her a mirror and her small purse, he pressed a soft kiss to her forehead and smiled down at her. "You look thoroughly sated, baby. Your hair is mused to perfection, your lips swollen from sucking my brother until his eyes crossed. And the flush covering your body will be a beacon to every Dom who sees you walk into the club. They'll all be jealous as hell." He chuckled when he saw her wince at her reflection. They were still several minutes from the club, so she had a few minutes to get herself together before they entered Dark Desires, and he and Peter could start messing her up again.

They were surrounded the minute they walked through the door, but Tobi and Gracie's happy shrieks were overshadowed by the stern looks of their Masters' faces. Kent's quick nod toward the hallway leading to the office didn't herald good news. They sent their subs to the ladies locker room with colorful warnings about what would happen if they ventured out before one of them returned for them, and then made their way to the office.

"I don't want to be a wet blanket, but I wanted you both to know this as soon as I knew. Anyway…Eric Roberts just sent me a video of Lara's parents getting off a plane in Jakarta. Officials there didn't detain them, even though they knew who they were. Rita Emmons straight up conned them, I swear if I didn't want to strangle her, I'd hire her." Kyle ran his hand through his hair in frustration before rolling his eyes, "Bottom line is, they are in the wind and we're all pulling back."

"Don't forget the bank." Fischer and Peter both turned their attention to where Jax stood shaking his head. "I agree with Kyle, they really need to hire that woman. She waltzed into the bank in a disguise that would have fooled God himself, sweet-talked one of the bank's newest employees into letting her into what was supposed to be a secured area, and promptly cleaned out the small cache we'd left—sans the micro-tracker. She left the small device with a note attached that said, 'Lame'." Laughing, the man inclined his head in his friend's direction, "Micah's pissed. He lost a five hundred dollar bet with Roberts over this."

Micah's muttered cursing came from the other side of the room, "I still can't believe she found it. Hell, it's not much bigger than a mustard seed. We need new toys when a damned government spook gets one up on us." Micah's words might have sounded as if he was pissed, but Fischer could hear admiration in his tone. Hell of it was, against his better judgement—he found himself admiring the woman as well.

Kent stepped forward, the resignation in his expression

was easy to read. "Cam is the only person who might have a chance of communicating with them. He called this morning to say he'd gotten a cryptic, anonymous email about taking care of former employees. Something about the way it was worded made him think it was about Lara. Evidently he had worked a couple of ops with the Emmons years ago so they would have known how to get in touch with him. But the bottom line is, other than trying to help and protect Lara, we have no reason to pursue her parents."

"And since I'm fairly certain Special Agent Roberts isn't laying all his cards on the table, we're backing out of it—at least for now." Kyle looked between Fischer and Peter, "I'm sorry about interrupting your evening, now let's get back out there. I'm sure our subs have managed to stir up enough trouble by now to keep the evening entertaining."

"Try to not beat on your sub's ass until after the ceremony—wouldn't want you to scare Lara off." Fischer laughed as they moved down the hall. He'd struggled to hold back his interest in Lara until his brother had finally come to Houston, and the truth was he still worried she might slip through their fingers so he was more than a little anxious to lock their permanent collar around her pretty neck.

The piece the jeweler created for them was an amazing combination of lifestyle elements concealed in what looked like a traditional choker. The elaborate design hid floggers, whips, and keys were just a few of the secrets incorporated into the scrolled pattern. People in the vanilla world would never notice all the symbolism, they would simply see an elaborate piece of jewelry with enough gold, diamonds, and sapphires to fund a small country for several years.

PETER PULLED LARA into his arms and kissed her soundly as soon as she stepped out of the lounge. She'd obviously had time to relax with her friends and the glow of laughter radiated all around her. Seeing her eyes sparkle with happiness and her sweetly rounded cheeks slightly flushed made his heart sing. He wasn't sure when he'd become such a sappy romantic, but everything felt right in his world when he held her.

Traditionally, the Doms at Dark Desires either fucked their subs on stage before collaring them or marked them with a single tail, but he and Fischer agreed neither of those was right for their fiancée. There might come a day when she was ready for that level of public play, but neither of them cared much one way or the other. The short ceremony they'd planned centered on her submission to them. Knowing how difficult it was for her to strip and be completely naked in public, they'd decided that would be the only thing they'd ask of her.

Turning her into his brother's arms, Peter heard Fischer whisper, "Come here, baby. I want to hold you for a minute." Peter heard Lara's soft sigh and the sound sent a surge of blood to his cock forcing him to shift in an effort to relieve some of the pressure. Having a permanent zipper imprint the length of his favorite body part wasn't something he was interested in. Fischer's smile over Lara's head let him know his younger brother was enjoying his discomfort.

'Not feeling any pity for you at all, big brother. As I recall, you've already enjoyed our pretty fiancée once this evening.' Anybody who thought younger brothers outgrew being a

pain in the ass had never met his. Unfortunately, this time Fischer was right and he needed to rein in his lust because throwing her over his shoulder and making a mad dash for nearest unoccupied room wasn't a part of tonight's plan.

They followed the Wests into the main room letting the two tall Doms block her view until they were close to the small raised platform they'd be using for the ceremony. Tobi and Gracie had spent weeks planning every detail of the decorations and their hard work had paid off beautifully. The leaf and branch garland that lay around the edge of the platform was woven with varying lengths of satin ribbon and soft white lights. There was a small white pillow in the center for Lara to kneel on and he was pleased to see it wasn't made of silk. He's seen subs struggle so hard to maintain their position when the pillow under them was slick, and he'd heard them say later they barely remembered the words that had been spoken to them because they were trying to avoid falling to the floor in a naked heap.

Seeing the velvet box he knew held her collar made Peter long to hurry the process along, but Lara deserved every bit of pomp and circumstance these ceremonies usually entailed. She might not see the value tonight, but as she watched other subs being collared in the future, he didn't want her feeling as though she'd been shortchanged. Kent and Kyle West each took a step to the side in what Peter was sure had been a well-planned move revealing the platform to Lara. He heard her sharp intake of breath followed by a shudder that he suspected was more about fear than arousal.

Peter and Fischer moved quickly turning Lara so her back was to the small stage and she faced them. "Baby? Talk to us. We thought this was something you would be happy about." Peter knew Fischer had barely been able to speak, fearing his worst nightmare was going to play out in front of almost every member of the club. The entire room was filled with members who had come to see the club's managers collar one of their favorite employees. He doubted Lara knew how popular she was with both her co-workers and the members of the club, but the fact they were probably breaking every fire code in the book should give her a good idea.

Peter watched as Lara opened her mouth and then closed it again several times without uttering a word. He saw the fear in her eyes, but he also saw something else—mentally holding Fischer back, he wanted her to ask for what she needed. "I'm scared. I need you…I need you to help me…help me focus." Her barely whispered words were drowned out by the whispers of those surrounding them, but he'd heard them.

He smiled at her, "Very good, I know that was really hard for you and I want you to know how pleased I am that you were honest." Stepping aside, he moved Lara to the very edge of the stage and sent Fischer a quick mental picture of what he had in mind. "Bend over and grab the edge of the platform." When she sucked in a quick breath, he crossed his arms over his chest and firmed his voice, "Now." She quickly bent over which made her dress pull up over the creamy cheeks of her ass displaying her nicely to the room. "Spread your feet a little further apart. We want another look at all that pretty pink flesh. We're going to paddle your ass until it's the same sweet color."

While Fischer started her spanking, Peter nodded to Kyle to proceed. Kyle flashed him a knowing grin and stepped to the middle of the platform to begin. Kyle welcomed everyone and briefly explained Lara had asked her Doms for their *help* getting her head in the right place for tonight's ceremony. Everyone laughed when he noted they'd graciously agreed to assist. By the time he and his brother had turned her ass a lovely pink her muscles had relaxed and Peter knew she'd let the sting of the swats push her fear aside.

Standing in the middle of the platform watching Lara slip her dress down over her clamped nipples and then over her hips before letting it fall softly at her feet was pure erotic wonder. She slid gracefully to kneel on the pillow spreading her knees wide and placing her hands on her thighs before tilting her chin down letting her golden curls fall forward. She looked like a Greek goddess and for several seconds Peter wasn't sure he was going to be able to adequately express how grateful he was for the gift of her trust.

"Lara, you have given us the most precious gift anyone can give another person. You have placed yourself in our hands, your trust honors us and we will cherish it always." Peter slid the choker around her neck and held one end as Fischer held the other.

"Lara, you are the light that reaches inside our souls, lighting every dark corner with your love and laughter. You've agreed to be our wife but agreeing to belong to us—to entrust us with your body and soul by wearing our collar is a commitment made soul-to-soul." Peter heard Lara's breathing speed up just as the first tears splashed on the top of her breasts. The salty drops rolled down the inside and outside curves before dropping silently on to her thighs.

"Do you accept our gift and agree to wear this collar as an outward symbol of your commitment to us? Do you agree to be our submissive, to abide by the rules we set for you, knowing everything we do is done with your best interest in mind?" Peter placed the fingers of his free hand under her chin tilting it up until he and Fischer could look into her eyes. "We'll build our lives around you, *mi amõre*. Your safety, health, and happiness will be at the core of every decision we make from this moment forward if you agree to wear our collar. What's it gonna be?"

Lara's eyes were a clearer shade of blue than he'd ever seen them and her tears vanished so quickly he had to blink to make sure he'd really seen the resolve that was now in her expression. "It will be my honor to wear your collar, Masters. I'll accept your gift and return it ten-fold in the pride I feel belonging to you." Her words had gone straight to his heart and Peter knew his brother felt the same. They didn't waste a moment locking the collar into place. He loved the fact the lock was hidden, no one would ever know where the key fit but Peter, Fischer, and the jeweler.

The entire room erupted into applause as they pulled Lara to her feet. They'd loosened the nipple rings earlier so they were little more than ornamentation at this point, so they didn't bother to remove them before sliding her dress back into place. The long kisses they gave her earned them shouts of approval and encouragement from someone in the back of the room, causing their sweet sub to flush crimson. A sight the brothers knew they would never grow tired of seeing in a lifetime with this woman.

The End

Books by Avery Gale

The Wolf Pack Series
Mated – Book One
Fated Magic – Book Two
Tempted by Darkness – Book Three

Masters of the Prairie Winds Club
Out of the Storm
Saving Grace
Jen's Journey
Bound Treasure
Punishing for Pleasure
Accidental Trifecta
Missionary Position

The ShadowDance Club
Katarina's Return – Book One
Jenna's Submission – Book Two
Rissa's Recovery – Book Three
Trace & Tori – Book Four
Reborn as Bree – Book Five
Red Clouds Dancing – Book Six
Perfect Picture – Book Seven

Club Isola

Capturing Callie – Book One

Healing Holly – Book Two

Claiming Abby – Book Three

I would love to hear from you!

Email:

avery.gale@ymail.com

Website:

www.averygalebooks.com/index.html

Facebook:

facebook.com/avery.gale.3

Instagram:

avery.gale

Twitter:

@avery_gale

Excerpt from Mated

The Wolf Pack
Book One
by Avery Gale

JAMESON WOLF HAD been almost ready to head home when he'd taken one last look out of the front windows of his office. Looking down over the sidewalk below, he wondered why the waiting line was so long on a frigid Friday night. He'd started to turn back to the room when his eye caught on a flash of red. Damn it to hell, he'd always had a thing for auburn haired women. Redheads were rare among shifters so he took a closer look. It might have been her long flowing mane of red curls that caught his attention, but there was something about her saucy attitude that drew him in. Watching her, he saw her easy rapport with the tiny blonde beauty she was with and he liked the fact that she seemed oblivious to the fact that she turned the head of every man near her.

Making his way down the steep circular staircase he was assailed by the overpowering scents of both humans and his peers who had braved the biting cold January night in the wind swept city. He saw the red-haired beauty enter through the heavy doorway a split second before the scent of his mate barreled over him. It was as if every neuron in his brain had been suddenly struck by lightning and was now crackling with electrical energy. His vision tunneled and his sole mission became to find the owner of that scent and mark her as his.

As he neared the red-haired beauty who had caught his eye earlier, the exotic fragrance he'd been following became more and more potent. *Could I actually be that lucky after all these years?* Stepping up behind her he took a deep breath letting her scent soak deeply into his soul. Even though he loved the fresh citrus smell of her hair, it was the essence of her that was nearly over-powering in its allure. It pulled him in and made every one of his senses come sharply into a pinpoint focus. He'd heard his friends describe this moment, but he had truly believed that their words had been little more than romantic folly—until now.

When she turned toward him, he became instantly aware that she'd been planning to escape. There was a look of panic in her eyes—what he didn't understand was what had spooked her. Awareness and anxiety were coming off her in heavy, crashing waves. He could smell fear in humans and shifters, but that wasn't what he was picking up. No, she wasn't afraid of him, but she wasn't thrilled to have been found either. *Interesting.* Mating scents are an almost overwhelmingly powerful draw for both male and female shifters so there was no doubt she had known her mate was near. So why was she trying to leave?

Both Jameson and his brother, Trevlon, were the Alphas of their pack and had been since their fathers were killed by rivals seven years ago. They had always known they'd follow pack tradition and share a mate, but they hadn't had any luck finding her despite having traveled all over the globe searching. *How has this beauty flown under our radar? She is exactly the type of woman we are both attracted to.*

"What is your name, beautiful?" Jameson knew his words had come out as more of a growl than a question, but considering how close he was to claiming her right here in the middle of the club, it was the best he could do. He relaxed a bit when he saw her deer in the headlights look. *Good – I'm happy to know she is as slammed by the attraction as I am.*

"Kit." He heard the wobble of nervousness in her voice and could tell she had barely been able to squeak out the word so he just waited. He saw her draw in a deep breath through her mouth and almost laughed at her ineffective attempt to avoid breathing through her nose. He tried to suppress his smile when she repeated the gesture because it was a futile attempt to escape the scent of her mate.

Once a shifter found their mate, their bodies were taken over by overwhelming sexual urges that lasted for weeks. He'd seen pack members all but disappear during that time because they could barely leave their bedrooms. He waited patiently as she finally seemed to come back to awareness and answered, "I mean, Kathleen, my name is Kathleen Harris." She was trying to look around him, which was amusing because she couldn't be more than five feet three or four inches tall and that was including the ridiculously high-heeled black leather stiletto boots she was wearing.

He was sure she hadn't meant to give him her nickname because it was likely something she reserved for those she considered close friends, so when he addressed her again, he used it deliberately. "Well, Kit, follow me, please."

He turned on his heel and started back toward the staircase when she reached out and grasped his forearm. "Wait, I can't go with you. I don't even know you. And my friend will be looking for me." The instant she touched him he'd felt a jolt of electricity arc between them and then tiny bolts of lightning streaked up his spine. *Damn, her touch did that through the fabric of his shirt, what would it feel like when they were skin to skin?*

The twin bond between him and Trev had always been incredibly strong, so he wasn't at all surprised when his phone rang. "Where are you? Are you okay?" Typical Trevlon, straight to it—he couldn't be troubled to utter a polite greeting.

"Standing in front of a woman I want you to meet. We're in the bar, but we'll be on our way upstairs as soon as we locate her friend to let her know where we are heading. Meet us in the office in five." Jameson disconnected the call and turned to one of his staff that was walking by. He quickly gave the man a detailed description of Kit's friend and instructions to stay close to her and keep her safe until she was ready to leave the building. At that time, he was to accompany her to the office. Jameson stood six foot seven inches tall in his boots, so he could easily see the tiny blonde on the other side dance floor and directed the young man to her. Jameson was glad it had been Charlie who'd been the first to walk by. He trusted the young shifter to do exactly as he'd been told.

Turning back to Kit, he realized for the first time that he had taken the hand she'd used to grab his arm and was holding it in his own. He'd been rubbing small circles over the inside of her wrist with his thumb. As his gaze met hers he felt her pulse speed up and watched as her pupils dilated. "Come along, Kit. We need to talk." This time he did smell fear so he pulled her into his arms and leaned down so his words would be painted over the soft shell of her ear like a warm brush of air, "I won't hurt you—ever. Be brave, sweet kitten."

Made in the USA
Columbia, SC
03 July 2017